Summertime Sprinkler

What do you do when the past moves in next door?

Pam Kumpe

Pam Kumpe

Copyright © 2022 Pam Kumpe

Cover Photo: Pam Kumpe

ISBN- 979-8-9855903-1-9

DEDICATION

For the weary traveler

He heals up the brokenhearted and binds up their wounds.
PSALM 147: 3 ESV

DISCLAIMER

Names, characters, businesses, places, events,
and incidents are either the products of the author's
imagination or used in a fictitious manner.

Any resemblance to actual persons, living or dead,
or actual events is purely coincidental.
This book is a work of fiction.

Pam Kumpe

A FLOOD OF THE HEART

One split second made me a widow while at the same time altering the life of a blue-eyed boy who lived next door. I've tried not to think about that afternoon for the past twenty years. But another anniversary comes every August. It's a day to get lost in regret and how I handled parts of the tragedy. It feels like the horror happened yesterday. Even now.

The little boy who once played in my yard, Hudson Hinkle, is thirty now, and his annual emails never bothered me until he moved back to New Boston a few years ago.

With so many states to live in and with the size of Texas, why did Hudson return to this town? It is beyond me. And yes, he lives some five blocks from my house.

I often wish the month of August away because Hudson takes me to the dreadful day when we both suffocated from the onslaught of suffering. His email will squeeze my emotions as if I'm trying on shoes, three sizes too small, forcing me to relive the accident.

I've tortured myself too much already, guilty of hitting the rerun button in my mind for about five years after the fateful day. And of course, I'm afraid I'll eventually bump into Hudson at the store, church, or the gas station. That's why I never drive my car down Merrill Street, even though it's a shortcut on the way to church. But if I don't go that way, I won't see Hudson's house, or car, or him.

Even now, I wonder if I'll ever completely heal or find victory over that horrible day in 2002. Some wounds leave permanent scars that no one sees. Other injuries from the past can bleed without permission and can break open like stitches when someone blames you for things out of your control. The monster of despair crashes into my life every summer—every August.

After the accident, I became a weary wanderer, ensuring my schedule remained full. Helping others, serving, and keeping my mind occupied assured me of no time for anything else. Then I won't spend hours looking back, wishing to change things, and worrying about Hudson.

In theory, that made sense—but in my real world, it's not working, and my mind races. My nightmares come. And I panic and deal with anxiety—yet I hide it for the most part from everyone else.

No matter what I do, I can't forget Hudson's ten-year-old face and his red eyes and the tears as he stood frozen in the spray of the water sprinkler in my backyard. No small boy should hear his mother scream as she learned of her husband's car accident from the policeman. The chain-link fence allowed Hudson to take in the entire conversation, while I charged to hold him on the grass—and he hit me for the first time that day and ran home in the cul-de-sac. Never to return. Never to play at my house again. Never to climb the oak tree where butterflies flit. And laughter abounds.

When I think the nightmares are gone, they show up again, only with the same characters. Those dreaded moments come when I'm sound asleep and always include the same three colors. Blue for sadness. Red for the anger Hudson harbors toward me. And purple because I'm annoyed at his pulling on my heartstrings like snapping a whip at me.

When I wake up, the panic swirls like there's a wild bull trapped in the comforter with me, and I feel like I'm being thrown in the middle of the rodeo arena. I'm sweaty and cold in my bed. Then I can't sleep at all.

I overthink small things, too, like finding my back door unlocked when I'm sure I fastened all three bolts before bed. It's as if clarity often escapes me, or so my old pastor, boss, and close friend, Stanley, says. He believes I'm distracted and forgetful. I keep telling him, I remember twisting those knobs and double-checking the latches. But still, some mornings, the door is unlocked anyway.

I've lived alone my entire adult life, except for two years of marriage. It was love at first sight when I met Rhett in the summer. We met at the pancake breakfast during the Pioneer Days Festival. He accidentally knocked my plate out of my hand and brought me another one with twice as many pancakes. I was nineteen. He was twenty-five. And we were married by Christmas. Our wedding took place in the morning so we could serve pancakes at the reception.

For almost two years, my friends thought I lived the dream of a perfect marriage, but the bruises beneath my shirt told another story. The trips to the doctor for a broken wrist and sprained ankle came with lies, when I said I tripped in my yard or on a rug. The cuts on my head, I explained away by lying too; by saying I'd bumped my noggin on a shelf in the storage building, the cabinet, or the low branch from our tree.

The doctors suspected. My friend, Sally Snow, questioned me. I'm sure the whispers were circling in our small town, but I hid the purple and blue and red marks from everyone. It became my daytime nightmare too—the secrets were almost as painful as a fist in the jaw.

But how many times would my face find Rhett's fist? How many times would I lock myself in the bedroom until he jimmied the lock? How many Sundays would I ask God to forgive me for telling lies when it went against my faith and my beliefs?

Then my life unraveled when Rhett played a part in taking the life of another man in a crash on Highway 82. He would pull his truck into a car driven by our neighbor, Hudson's father, Peter Hinkle—grief upon grief. Little Hudson lost his smile. I already lost mine—goodness, there's no easy solution to finding a way to smile again after such horror.

**

On my couch, I leaned forward and touched the keyboard on my laptop. I looked at my computer screen, ready to open the email that would take me back twenty years to when life exploded like a volcano of scorching anguish. I pulled my hand away from the trackpad. "No, not this time. I'm not reading your email, Hudson Hinkle. Not this year."

The latest email landed in my inbox yesterday, the notification popping up on my cell phone. So last night I was fidgety and full of runaway thoughts —a blur of red, blue, and, yes, the painful purple. Those notes sent me down the road to my horrible day, to Hudson's equally painful day, but I'm not opening the email. Or so I keep saying. The notes from him are too much; Hudson rehashes the horror, real and vivid—and I get stuck with the images of his loss—and of seeing the two caskets. It's unhealthy to keep digesting his pain with mine.

It's as if I keep checking the horizon, though, and like I'm standing on the bow of a boat, hoping the waves don't crash over me. I can see the sun, the ball of yellow calling me to a new life. To one with purpose. Where ashes give way to joy.

But the wounds of that frantic afternoon have bled with too many unresolved issues far too long, and the answers won't come. The ones we have won't solve anything either.

But no matter, I can't thoroughly shake off the impending doom or understand why my goodbye to Rhett left two people dead on that Sunday afternoon.

Knock. Knock. Knock.

I placed my mango tea on the coffee table and closed my laptop. "I'm coming. I need a ride to work. My car is sputtering and wishing it were in the junkyard. I'm ready to have it towed and buried there." I called Stanley on the other side of the front door. I turned the lock, flipped the two deadbolts, and unhooked the chain.

I'm determined that no one gets inside my house without an invitation, and the extra locks help me breathe. Besides, if anyone did bust in, I'd hear the commotion and have time to hide or run. The recent break-ins in my part of town have added to my uneasiness, too.

Knock. Knock. Knock.

"Just a second, Stanley." I pulled the door open, and Beauty pressed her kitty nose on the screen while I pushed it wide. "Wait, Colt? What are you doing here? And how did you get here?" I opened the screen wider, glancing at the road for a car. I then bent down, getting close to the small boy. "What are you up to?"

Colt's snaggletooth grin lit up my heart. "Ms. Beth, I lost my paper."

"But how did you get here? Or know where I lived?" I questioned the bus-riding newcomer to Children's Church who had joined the choir.

He pointed to his bike in the front yard. "I rode here. I don't need training wheels either."

I rattled my brain with images. "Wait, did you just move into the vacant house behind me? I've noticed a moving truck there the last couple of days."

"Uh-huh. We moved in yesterday from across town. Mom said my church choir teacher lived on the other side of the wooden fence by our driveway, so I came over and knocked on your door. I can't find the words to my song."

"I'm so glad you're my neighbor. That house has been vacant for too long." I smiled at my newest member in the children's choir, one who's ridden the church bus from south of town. "Just a minute. I have another copy or two in my bag. I'll be right back."

I rushed to my office down the hallway, grabbing the sheet music from my satchel, an old leather tote given to me by Stanley. I twirled around and bumped right into Colt. "Oh, hey there. So come on in."

"I did. Your cat meowed, so I picked her up. She's solid black." Colt petted Beauty, and she purred a song of contentment.

"She's a stray from way back when." I handed him the sheet of music. "Here you are. You have plenty of time to learn the words. We're doing the back-to-school program in a few weeks."

Colt put Beauty down by my feet, skipped out the door, and went to the front porch. "Thank you. Bye."

I held the screen. "See you Sunday."

I stepped outside and to the porch, leaning forward. I looked left and watched as Colt peddled his bicycle to the house behind me, the paper flapping in the wind as he held onto it.

He glanced back, wiggling as he rode. "Bye. Thanks for my song." His blue and red bike slipped behind the corner of my house, but then, like lightning, it came back into view. "Ms. Beth, your sprinkler is flooding the street."

I barreled across the driveway. "Thank you. I'd forgotten I left the water running. August brings nothing but dead grass, and I love green. It's a sign of life. I probably use my sprinkler more than most people. But I'm glad you noticed. My water bill is high enough."

After circling the corner and back, Colt waved. "Bye, Ms. Beth. I'm going to practice my song."

I smiled and turned off the water faucet; the trickle of water lessened and stopped. I stepped into the street, facing the cul-de-sac. "Bye, it's great to have you."

Stanley's truck pulled in front of the house, his eyes jumping from their sockets as he tried to see what I was doing. He rolled his window down. "Hurry, Gladys and Reed are ready to call it a day at the station. What's wrong with your Accord now?"

"It's leaking oil. It's sputtering. It's an unhappy car." I wiped my wet hands on my jeans. "Let me get my satchel and my tea."

Stanley called, "You'd better get your cat. She'll wander off if you leave her outside."

I marched past my Honda, the car I've driven for nearly thirteen years, and petted the hood and announced, "I believe in getting my money's worth; she's been a good ride. But her burial is long overdue." I slipped my hands under Beauty, went inside, grabbed my tea, and my folder with my talk-show notes. "See you later, sweet Beauty. Watch over the house."

As I rushed to Stanley's Chevy pickup, I sighed deeply, and the memory of Rhett jumped into my head, taking over my thoughts. He drove a pickup like Stanley's, but it was newer, cleaner, and faster. I wiped my brow, the heat of summer unraveling my past like flashcards.

I held onto the handle of the truck, thinking about how Rhett left while I wept and screamed on the front porch, shouting for him to go while at the same time, praying he'd stay. I was conflicted in my desires, my anger longing to subside, my heart wishing for peace. I wanted to show grace, but at what cost? There was a certain amount of relief when Rhett started the truck. I figured he'd return in a day or two, and I'd forgive him again, and the cycle of abuse would return. The current bruises would fade, only to pop up in a new place, like my back, neck, or stomach.

Rhett backed out of the driveway, the tires spun, and the pickup painted the asphalt with his goodbye. I'd exploded into a broken faucet of tears, flooding the street with my cries while hoping I was wrong to let him leave. To push him away. I'd expected to see his truck in front of the house or coming down Hall Street within minutes after he left—the cycle of our broken relationship spinning out of control. He yells. Hits me. And leaves. And usually, he comes back.

I waited. My fears turned into a puddle of sorrow and engulfed me. I became a pillar of salt, frozen, and I couldn't picture myself alone. Yet I've been alone for most of my life. My parents deserted me and left me in an abandoned house when I was three. One night, a woman saw me sitting on the front porch in only my undies and rescued me. I grew up in foster homes that were some safe and good, others were marginal.

But at twenty-one, I didn't want to be alone or divorced, or the talk of the town. At least, with Rhett's name attached to the horror.

Figuratively, the word *alone* became my middle name, except when talking to the callers on my radio show. Not that I have many callers. They're my tribe, as the younger folks say.

But when I do get calls on my talk show, that's when I offer hope—offer light into the night. I long to show grace to other broken souls who fight for joy. I look for the heart that is standing on the bow, looking at the horizon, lost in the waves of despair. Yes, many are trapped by their choices and or caught in a cycle that needs to be watered with reason, clarity, and hope.

**

If there's one thing I've learned, now that I'm forty-one, it's that I'm not the only wanderer. But one question still haunts me. "Why couldn't I fix my marriage?"

All my life, my mind has run wild like hogs on a chase, especially when I go to bed. And if I stayed home too much, the depression would take over. So, when Stanley invited me to host the talk show at the radio station where his wife, Gladys, and their good friend Reed worked, I jumped at it.

I left the world of retail and fell in love with radio. I love encouraging others, teaching Children's Church, leading the children's choir, and leading quarterly Bible studies for women at the church.

Those outlets give me a chance to lift others. At the station, since I talk to people who have insomnia and relentless overthinking, it allows me a way to point others to Christ, too, especially when circumstances mount. Trials drown us, like on days when the sprinkler of pain runs like a faucet left on too long.

Everyone is treading on water, so to speak, and some barely have a nostril above the water. And they feel like they're sinking. With hope, we can walk again, despite our past. And even swim.

Back then, I felt like I'd failed in my vows, the untold story of anger and fits of rage behind closed doors, almost like a nightmare—but real. It was the part of the ugly that no one heard me talk about, except for Sally, my dear friend. I told her much later, though—after the accident.

I'd married a man set loose to destroy me, well, on certain days. His demons targeted me whenever he lost the battle for peace. But he promised to change. He meant it when he said it. He'd make those pancakes and wash the dishes. Then go to the liquor store once more.

Then the hollow eyes returned, the frenzy of chaos overtook his actions, and his fists lost control. The blows pounded me, ripping away my joy, causing me to try to stay out of his way. Sometimes, I didn't get away. There were more of those days than the ones where I escaped his wrath.

And that's when I started watering the grass, watching for new life, and hoping something would grow from the brown color.

So, on that fateful afternoon, my husband packed his bags and marched out the door, right after holding me against the wall in a chokehold. He declared at that moment he had to protect me from his inner demons. I agreed he should leave, shaking on the inside. So much for marital bliss.

Stanley interrupted my wandering disappearance down the broken memory of sorrow. "Beth Bender, get in this truck. We've got to go."

Startled, I quivered and swallowed hard, my hand stuck on the truck's handle as I stood in the road. "Sorry. I got lost in the past. And besides, my show doesn't even start until 10 p.m. I'll get the other devotionals and commercials recorded before then. It's not even five."

Stanley mumbled, his dentures clapping in his mouth. "Gladys hates to be kept waiting. You know that makes her mad."

"Goodness, she knows you're late for church and everything. You've been married a million years. She never gets mad at you; she's a softy. But she will make sure she finds more work for us to do."

Clutching the steering wheel, Stanley inched around the corner, and we passed a white sedan, driving way too fast.

I threw out my two cents. "Doesn't that guy know this is a residential neighborhood? Children are playing."

Stanley grimaced, "I'm not touching that one. You don't even want to know who was driving that car."

RECORDINGS OF THE PAST

Stanley pulled into the radio station's gravel lot on Daniel's Chapel Road, parking next to the old sedan driven by Gladys. The station was built beside the rodeo arena way back, sometime before I was born. The place where horses, bulls, and cowboys ride and learn their craft. I've learned my craft at the station, too, although it seemed I was bouncing off the bull at times. My learning curve was complex. But I'd get up again and, on my feet, only to get tossed to the ground again. I just kept standing up. I was determined not to give up.

Since yesterday's email, the constant overthinking feels like ten bulls were set loose in my brain. Maybe if I'd opened the email, perhaps I could move on and stop the circle of regrets and lost steps. I wondered what the email said. And I can't stop thinking about opening it.

I can't stop imagining the scene of what it must have looked like when Rhett pulled onto the main highway, speeding right toward the interstate by Denny's. Witnesses said he charged through the intersection on Hwy 98, and at the red light, he turned left, slamming into the driver's side of a car, injuring Peter.

Peter was headed home from a day of fishing with his buddies and never had a chance to get out of the way. The wreck happened about three miles from our cul-de-sac. And just like that, two men were hanging on for life by a thread. One that snapped within a couple of hours when both men succumbed to their injuries.

I sighed, remembering how my husband would never hit me again. Or choke me. Or yell. Or push me. Or send me to the doctor for stitches, where I'd lie about how the abrasions and broken bones happened. And oddly, his death brought relief layered with immense sorrow. To think, I thought his death was a good thing, which then made me worry for years about what a terrible person I must be.

I hated feeling that way, yet I'd never get a handle on why the rage exploded inside his heart either. I'd never have the opportunity to see if we'd have children or find a fresh start. I'd never sing again in the adult choir at church or sing specials. After that day, I stopped singing until I was drafted to lead two children's choir groups. Singing along with the kids was better than having no song to sing of my own.

When I first learned it was Peter that Rhett collided with, the shock made me overwater my yard for months. I bought every sprinkler I saw at the store. And I flooded the grass, the street, even my neighbor's yard. Maybe the pain would wash down the curb and go away.

In the blink of an eye, Hudson's dad would never play basketball with him either. Or toss a baseball. Or take him fishing. Or tuck him into bed. Or kiss him. Or wish him a happy birthday. Any relief I felt was exchanged for grief as I thought about the loss of Hudson's memories with his father. The purple maze of horror made my chest explode, my breath shallow, my inability to cope grew with the years, and I stayed in constant turmoil.

I've tried to sort through the questions, not every day, but on each anniversary for sure. It's one of the saddest days of my life. If I had stopped Rhett, Hudson's dad might be alive. If I had hidden the keys or the bottle of vodka, my husband wouldn't have caused the accident. But would I have survived the next blow to my head if he'd stayed? Or the next chokehold? How many times could a fist hit my jaw before I collapsed from the impact?

So, giving back became my goal, and a bit of me heals in the process, too. I love offering hope to my callers on my talk show by sharing comforting verses from the Bible. I also record my podcasts from home, sharing stories to provide insight into overcoming the emotional baggage we carry in life. I over-prepare for my Children's Church class and my women at church. I know every song by heart that the kids sing in the choir. I overdo and overprepare. I don't sit still well.

On that Sunday back in 2002, I was supposed to sing in the service, but once I started crying, I didn't stop for weeks. I no longer could find a reason to sing. Although at times, I do hear myself humming—enjoying the rejoicing that rings in my heart as if the musical notes trapped in my lungs longed to escape.

I'm a friend on my talk show, and we have conversations that bring insight as we seek God's guidance. All a person has to do is call my talk show on KNBO. I'm on the air Monday through Friday, from ten to midnight, before the last of the community falls to sleep, where the lonely and hurting might need someone to talk to, which is me, Beth Bender. Your friend. And your neighbor.

Unexpected tragedies in life can help you find a mission field to bless others, but finding the light often means enduring terrible darkness until you can see again. Well, that's how it plays out for me, even as I face the past that captures my thoughts today.

I watched Hudson grow up without his father for the next few years. I should have moved since they lived behind me. But money was tight. Options were few. Living took over. Time got away.

I noticed Hudson became angry with me and threw rocks from his driveway. He shot the birds on my feeder with his pellet gun. And he aimed at the squirrels, too. He knocked over my trash can on the street when it was packed. I'd start my water sprinkler; he'd turn it off. I'd turn the water on again, and he'd slip into my yard, unhooking the sprinkler from the water hose.

It's safe to say Hudson held his breath the day his dad died and allowed the unresolved rage to explode into mischievous expressions of sorrow.

I lost track of Hudson around the age of fifteen when he went away to live with his uncle in Arkansas. Then my sprinklers were left alone, and my orange cat, Brassy, stopped throwing up. I often wondered if Hudson gave her molded leftovers or worse. But she lived another year after he moved, which showed how paranoid I'd become.

After the wreck, Hudson always petted Brassy when I wasn't looking, and he kissed her ear. He wasn't mad at her. And yet, I thought the worst when she got sick.

When I'd heard that Hudson had moved back here in his late twenties, I went stupid again, found him on social media, and blocked his page. I needed space. And I needed to walk my path. Or so I tried—but I was bound to run into him eventually.

My cat, Beauty, replaced Brassy, and she has outlived every season of my ups and downs. She must have more than nine lives because she's hanging in there with me. However, she does sleep more, has fewer excursions at night, and cuddles whenever she can. I tell her everything. And she never judges me. I sure wish cats gave out advice.

So yes, yesterday, August 1, 2022, a Monday, marked the anniversary week of the wreck, and Hudson emailed me once again. The unfortunate date was August 4th, but he sends the email every summer at the beginning of the month. He likes to torment me with his consistent and inappropriate emails.

And usually, in a quick stroke on my keyboard, I'll send scriptures in response to the rant. Hudson won't reply. And we'll be done for another year. But the damage to my spirit gets heavier with each passing summer.

I spoke to Stanley while stuck in my seat, sweat making my top stick to the upholstery. "I've got to take my thoughts captive and not fall into the pit again."

Stanley announced, "I'm going to take you captive. Stop the daydreaming and get out of the truck."

I sighed, exhaling a host of worries into the air. "Sorry, Stanley. I'm everywhere today. I do need to take my thoughts captive if I can find a switch to stop the noise."

Stanley opened my door. "In the Bible, Joseph's brothers may have tossed him into a pit when their emotions got the best of them, but Joseph refused to let the pit consume him. So come on. We've got work to do."

"Yes, I'm coming. Work calls." I froze, making eye contact with a horse by the fence.

Stanley tapped my shoulder. "Seriously! Standing and staring at that horse won't get your work done. We have commercials to record."

"Sorry, I'm struggling today. Goodness, if it were that easy to miss the pit, we'd all have a great life. And now, I've spent the last ten minutes of our drive to work rehashing a husband who hurt me and the car crash that took people away."

Stanley walked with me to the front of the station. "The noise inside you is too much. I pray the Lord quiets you and gives you peace."

I whispered, "Lord, please silence the past and bring healing. And do it for Hudson, too. We're both hurting. He thinks he's alone. I often do too. But I want to know your heart, Lord. If I can share any of what You've taught me, on persevering, on trusting You, let me share that with Hudson."

Stanley held the door open. "Excuse me, will I need to send you home? Are you fit to hold a talk show tonight?"

"Yes, I'm good. Perfect. I'm here. I've studied my Bible, and I'm ready to record and talk to the world tonight." I pushed my bangs aside, a few gray hairs hiding under the blonde. I followed Stanley inside, wondering if I'd get the chance to sprinkle hope into Hudson's life. Will we find a way to heal? Will the stigma of our loss give way to beauty for ashes?

Since Hudson lives on the other side of town, down a street I avoid, I'm pleased his mom's old brick house behind me is now occupied. I love children, so having Colt next door, who is curious and has the cutest dimples, made my afternoon today. I can't wait until the day he runs through my sprinkler, and I get the chance to share a little hospitality with him, like mango tea. Or maybe a root beer. Or a slice of my chocolate cake.

Colt reminds me of Hudson Hinkle, though, so surely not —surely Colt isn't his son. I tossed out the idea—only to retrieve the thought. Then I argued with myself, going back and forth. There are a lot of small boys in town. I heard someone at church say Colt's last name, but with all the children in the choir talking nonstop, I can't remember it now.

I spoke to myself out loud. "Beth Bender, stop acting like this. You're reacting like someone afraid. Colt isn't a Hinkle. He's not."

I discarded the idea for good and tossed it aside, happy to have a new neighbor boy next door.

I won't see Colt in his driveway, though, because I hired a man to build a wooden fence not long after the tragic accident, ripping out the chain link. A wooden wall could block the past. And the view. That way, Hudson's mom didn't have to look at me. After all, my husband left her a widow, too. It helped. Some. And then, after Hudson lived with his uncle and went off to college, his mother passed away from a heart attack on her way to his graduation. More sorrow. Such sadness. Loss happened at every turn.

I slapped Stanley on the back as we marched down the hallway. "Hey, who was driving the white car we passed by my house? You made an odd remark about it. You rolled your eyes, too."

"Never mind. It's not important. We have work calling us. And we're late."

I sighed, "We're always late."

**

I pressed him for an answer in Stanley's office and placed my hands strategically on his desk. "What's the deal? Why won't you tell me who that man was in the car?"

"Beth, it's not necessary to speak to me as if I'm a child. I can hear you. I can tell you what I want when I want. Or not at all. Let's just leave it alone."

"I'm not good at that. You must give me a clue." I put my hands on my hips.

Stanley held out a stack of paper. "Sorry, not today. Work calls. And right now, it's not important. Here are the three commercials. I've written them up for you. Bibles from the bookstore are on sale. A software company that helps you study your Bible is having an online clearance sale. And a gift store near Hooks is trying to get the word out about their new place. Record each of them and change up the tone a little. Not too perky. And not dreary. Use some of your drama to make them interesting. All three of these need to be finished before you go live tonight. Reed's running those commercials tomorrow."

"Sure thing, Captain." I saluted Stanley, so I could see his eyebrows disappear into the wrinkles on his forehead.

"Beth, if you weren't like a daughter, I'd fire you for your disrespectful tone with me."

"Disrespectful? Reed calls you Captain. You're the one who dishes it out; I'm just playing catch-up."

"I'm not Captain. He calls me that because of my high school baseball days. Just a plain old station manager or my name will do."

"You remember high school? That was like, a thousand years ago."

"I remember more than you realize, like the anniversary date of the wreck. And how on the show last night, you barely offered more than a few words to your callers. You were like a lost kitten searching for your momma. And today is not any better."

"I'm fine. This will subside in a day or so. It gets to me sometimes." I held the papers, waving them like paper airplanes. Sally and I will go shopping tomorrow. We're buying a new garden hose so she can keep her sunflowers alive. You know Stanley, I want to be like Sally when I grow up."

"Beth Bender! You're a forty-year-old woman. You need to be like you. The Lord made one, Beth. Be you. And since you asked."

I interrupted. "I didn't ask."

"Too late, I'm giving you some advice. Remember, you weren't responsible for the wreck. Not one bit."

"Easier said than done, Captain." I took the rest of the papers from his hand and scooted my feet toward the soundproof booth where we tape our messages. The small room blocks the sound, which I wish I could do with the speakers blaring inside my mind.

I peeked back into Stanley's office. "Sorry, I'm a mess, but I'll be fine. I promise. And I'll be back within ninety minutes or so. Then I'll record the daily devotionals for next week."

"Perfect. I'll let Reed go home, and I'll take his place on air. KNBO doesn't run itself."

I argued, "It nearly does."

Stanley rose, following me, and bumped his belly on the door jam, pointing his finger at me. "See, I get no respect around here."

Gladys danced into the narrow hallway, humming. "Now, don't let the old geezer get too big for his britches. He's never going to fire you. You're the glue for this station. He's got a birthday coming up. Eighty will look good on him, but we need some younger blood to follow in our shoes. Since his retirement, he's worked here so long that he can barely see the computer keys. And his hearing is worse than ever. And Reed's not far behind him."

Reed popped into the hallway, passing Stanley as they exchanged spots. Stanley shut the door to the booth where the action happened on air. Reed mouthed, "I heard that; see, I can hear."

Gladys wrapped herself around Reed, who stood three feet higher than most people. Or so it seemed. "Reed, I put the chicken spaghetti in the fridge. Now take it home. You've got supper. Just warm it up a bit."

Reed grinned; his crooked teeth, yellowed by his smoking days, seemed brighter as his eyes beamed with hope. "Ms. Gladys, I'm grateful as always."

She marched to the front of the station. "Stanley won't eat leftovers, so I've got to pass them on to someone."

I hollered. "I love chicken spaghetti. What about me?"

She bellowed with a cackle. "You have a container too."

I laughed, following Gladys to the front door. "Hey, where's my hug?"

"Sorry. "She turned back, embracing me with all her wrinkles, and those in her face stuck to my cheek. Those in her neck tried to hold onto my chin, and they hung like spaghetti, and her wrinkles beneath her clothes bounced off my skinny body, causing me to do a two-step and skip three times for balance.

Gladys moved to the parking lot, sliding into the driver's seat of her car, but before she shut the door, she called, "See you tomorrow. Reed's working the weekend, too. He's training some of the church's youth. Maybe a few of them will take over for us one day. They love technology."

I rushed to her side, skidding to a stop, not saying a word, a tear rolling down my face.

Gladys reached for my hand and stood up. "What's on your heart, pretty girl?"

"I'm just in a bad place today. I can't seem to concentrate. Can I get one more hug?"

Gladys unfolded, bouncing like Jell-O, and reached for my neck. "Sure thing, we all need hugs."

The reassurance of love from someone who cares about me despite my moodiness meant the world to me. Gladys gets me. She may be in her late seventies, but she's like a loose-skinned toddler. Gladys is fun, faithful, and the best cook in the county, too. Plus, a hug from the most gracious woman in town is always welcome. She plans the meals at the church and might boss folks a little, but we do eat well with her in charge.

As she got into the car and waved, she rolled down the window. "I heard you have new neighbors. I hope that hasn't upset you too much."

PROLONGED ANGER

I waved at Stanley through the soundproof glass where he punched keys and kept the radio station on the air. He's done his best to keep up with technology, challenged by computers, but determined to master them. I held up my sheets of paper, mouthing, "The recordings are waiting for you, Mr. Captain."

Stanley grinned, apparently reading my lips, and gave me a thumbs-up.

The last several hours took the breath out of me—so much for my promptness in making recordings. Each commercial required four or five takes due to my stuttering and forgetting where I was, which meant starting over more times than I wished.

I signaled with my hand as if I held a fork. "I'm going to eat my chicken spaghetti. Do you want some?"

Stanley shook his head, his eyes rolling up and his lips frowning.

"I'll take that as a no. I've got about thirty minutes until I go on air."

I marched down the long hallway to where day-old coffee sat in the pot, still warming, and remembered the station gets locked at seven—a rule Stanley insists on. I forgot to do it this evening due to the retakes.

I answered Stanley as if he were reminding me for the umpteenth time. "I'm going. I took so long in the recording booth; I'd better lock the front door before the night's monsters invade our station." I hurried up front, where headlights blasted me like a spotlight through the glass. I put my hand up, peeking under my hand-visor, and saw a car sitting next to Stanley's pickup. "Who is that? And why not come on in?"

I pushed open the door as the vehicle backed up, and the man in the driver's seat rolled his window down, his face shadowed by night.

He tossed a wadded piece of paper to the ground. "Keep this. Colt won't be needing it. He's not allowed to come over. Understand?"

The way he slurred his growl at me was a reminder of a voice from my past. "Wait! Hudson? Is that you?" My chest bone cracked with an ache as if it snapped. And the pounding in my head was as if a piece of my heart broke off and traveled to my brain. "Is that you? I don't know why you're talking about the boy in my choir. What have I done?"

Hudson yelled, "You gave him sheet music to learn a song. Don't talk to my kid."

"No! Colt, is your son? But he came over. I didn't seek him out." I coughed, my argument with Hudson going nowhere but in circles. "I didn't know Colt was your son. So, wait! You're my new neighbor?" I nearly choked on that question, wishing it were untrue, knowing it was.

"We are, and not by choice."

"No way, you've moved back into your mother's house behind me. And Colt with his dimples and blonde hair? He's your … your son?" My ramblings annoyed Hudson: his glare and tapping fingers on the steering wheel made it clear that I should stop asking questions. "I'm shocked, that's all. I met Colt at church, and I couldn't remember his last name. He looks like you—I knew it deep down. But I didn't want to admit it."

Hudson revved the motor. "I've had my say. Just stay away from my family."

I crumpled to the gravel, unable to move, my life rocked by the man who now lived on the other side of the backyard fence.

As a boy, Hudson made me so sad after the wreck. Now, he's grown and has moved in behind me! The endless horror of a tragedy is on replay once more.

I screamed, "Who does that? Why? I can't do this anymore!" I rocked on my heels and lost myself in the downpour of pain, slapping my temples with a hard pulse, the pressure in my lungs tight, and I felt dizzy. I held my chest, a giant boulder pressed on my neck, shooting a pain down my spine. My shoulder throbbed, and my eyes burned with the dust from Hudson's skidding tires. The sheet of music lay at my feet.

The white car disappeared down the highway as Hudson drove away, leaving me in the parking lot alone. After a few minutes, I gathered myself, only to stumble over the broken planter on the front walkway by the door. I scraped my shin across the sharp edge, cutting my pants. "Oh, gosh. Now I've gone and cut my leg."

Inside, I locked the door with a twist of the knob and hurried to the break room, where I dug through a drawer for Band-Aids. "Finally, here's a box." I sat in the chair next to the coffee pot, the smell of burnt brew almost enough to make me throw up. I rolled up my pants leg and taped eight Band-Aids over the gash. I never go to the doctor unless I'm bleeding to death, and tonight won't be that night unless my heart bleeds into my lungs and suffocates me.

I glanced up. "Lord, when will this be over? I can't keep doing this. I've put a Band-Aid on my heart, waited for the annual email, and now Hudson lives behind me? Why would he live there? His past haunts him. And now he's planning to haunt me in person."

My tears backed up, only to drop like rain onto the Band-Aid wrappers on the tile floor. I peeked at the clock. "Oh, my word. Now Stanley's going to show up. He's got the commercials going and a piece of trivia playing on the radio. He's probably on his way back here to get me."

I stood, picked up the wrappers, wiped my face with a paper towel, and sighed, "Get it together. Or Stanley's going to send you home."

From behind me, he answered, "That's right, it's time. Time for Beth Bender, our friend and neighbor. You have five minutes to airtime." Stanley twisted his eyes, his one eyebrow twitching. "Beth, are you going to make it?"

"Sure, Stanley. Lock up when you leave and get me at midnight. You can count on me."

"What happened to locking up the station at seven? I saw you go by the front through the window."

"I didn't get it done. I guess I just forgot."

"You didn't forget. You're preoccupied and unfocused. Maybe you should go home."

"No, I'm fine. This will be good for me. I need to talk to folks."

Mr. Frumpy unfolded his three bellies, shaking his head. "You could rest tonight. With all the recordings, the radio station is on remote. Taped sermons. Devotionals. Newsreels. Commercials on reels. Recorded music. You're the only live show we offer, except for Reed's commentaries. But even superheroes need rest."

"I'm not a superhero. I'm a woman who's gotten warped into her past and can't get back to the present."

"See, you do need rest."

"No, sir. I'm ready." I swallowed hard; the shivers of pain in my shin felt like knives stabbing at random intervals. I rubbed my leg; my jeans were stained with blood.

Stanley bent his head. "What happened?"

"Oh, nothing. I cut myself shaving my legs today."

"That's more than I need to know."

I sighed, "Well, you asked."

Stanley scratched his lip. "Beth, you know if the owner doesn't renew our license, our doors may close forever."

"Stanley, you've told me that forever. You own this place. You love to get my blood pressure up. I need this gig. It's where I find peace." I yanked out my papers from my satchel. "Look, I've taken notes from the Psalms today. I'm trying to find words to share, so you must renew the license. This is what I do. It's what I know."

Stanley turned off the coffee maker, rinsed the pot in the sink, and opened the trash lid, tossing the stinky coffee grounds from the filter into the packed container. "It's time to put some things out by the curb. Everything has its season. We're running an old station. People don't listen to the radio nowadays. We're not reaching the community. We're outdated and old."

"I'm not that old. We can turn this station around and make improvements. Gladys said Reed is training some younger people to learn the business."

"She's hoping we don't have to close or sell out. But since I retired as pastor last year, even the church has a new voice. And a younger leader. I'm getting up in age. I've kept this station on the air since the '80s, and it's time to close that chapter of my life."

I stomped around Stanley like a toddler. "What? You can't shut this place down. What are you saying?"

"It's time. At the end of the year, we're closing the doors. Enjoy the next few months."

I blocked Stanley from leaving the break room. "Then let me pay to renew the license. I'll buy the station from you. I can bring in new shows. We can revamp the equipment and reach a new audience along with my listeners."

"Beth, you don't have an audience. In the last few weeks, you've answered the phone less than ten times."

I waved my arms. "You're exaggerating. I've taken more calls than you know. And I talk to people. I share the Bible. I tell stories. Jesus was a storyteller. Let me tell His stories."

"Yes, you're a good talker. That's for sure."

I rushed to my booth to prepare for my show, and I glanced back. "This isn't over. I'm not leaving this place. I can't stop coming here. This is my home. I've given you so many years of my time. I've invested my life here. It's not wasted. It's not over."

Stanley shrugged his shoulders. "Beth, I'll lock up the front on my way out. Make plans. You must find something else to do. You have your podcast. You can do that and stay at home. We're closing the doors unless something changes."

I yelled, "I don't want to stay home. That won't pay my electricity bill or water bill."

"If you'd stop watering your yard every day, you could save some money. I heard they need help at the grocery store," Stanley argued, and then offered me the opportunity. "If you want this station, then prove to me that your show matters. And we'll talk more."

I planned my strategy, not sure what I could do—but Reed's great with such things. I'll get with him tomorrow.

For now, it's time for my show, if I can keep myself focused, and if I don't bleed to death from the cut on my leg.

TALK SHOW HAVOC

I mumbled words beneath my breath while placing my notes on the desk, positioning myself to greet the listeners I hoped would call in tonight. I mouthed my words to Stanley through the glass window in front of me, where he stood on the other side, waving goodbye. I slipped on my headset, whispering, although Stanley couldn't hear me. "In the blink of an eye, you think you can sell this place. It's a part of who I am. I belong here. This season isn't over. Not yet!"

I hit the button on the computer, speaking into my microphone, changing my tone to a higher-pitched one with less growl, one less accusing, and I hid my suffering soul with a mask of contentment. "Good evening, New Boston. Welcome to the show. This is Beth Bender. Your friend. And your neighbor. What's on your mind tonight? Let's talk. Just give me a call."

I tapped the table with my pencil, making small talk and sharing a silly story about getting lost in church as a girl. I went up some stairs and fell into the baptistry, which was full of water for a baptism. "Yes, folks, some days you get wet and nearly drown. But then it's time to come up for air. And dry off.

And next thing you know, you'll find your way to living your life with purpose."

I giggled at my memory of swimming in the baptistry and laughed into the mic. "Do any of you find that your past gets tossed in front of you as if you're never going to walk with hope? Do you suffocate as if you're drowning? We'll, I'm here to remind you that God is with you in the falling and in the rising."

I could have drowned or broken my leg as a girl in church that day. I choked on my words, the stinging in my shin throbbing with a constant tinge. And I couldn't stop thinking about seeing Hudson outside earlier.

My words went out to those listening to the show, but I needed to apply my own principles to my own life. "Well, folks, does anyone have a great story to share with me about your baptism?"

I nearly missed the blinking light on the phone line. I reached for the button and pressed down, but the dial tone told me the caller was already gone.

"Well, folks, I've given you the book of Psalms for the past hour. Life can be like a giant pasture. Full of weeds. Holes. Brown spots. And yet, fertile ground awaits. Let's remember the Lord is our Shepherd. He's the way and the truth. He's the giver of life. Now, if you're awake and you have a question for me, dial that phone."

My eyes fell to the four buttons, no lights—just emptiness and quietness. "Wait, listeners. There's a flashing light on line one. Yes, this is Beth Bender. Bend my ear. Share your question. Let's spend a few minutes and seek the Lord for guidance."

"Yes, this is Stanley. I forgot to take out the trash. Will you do it before you leave?"

"Stanley, don't take up this line. Someone needs a sunrise of hope tonight."

"Just take out the trash. Thanks. Don't forget."

I set the computer's dial to a two-minute recorded prayer and sent it over the airwaves. I wished for one call to make tonight count, and I talked to the walls with my mic off.

Since the piped commercial would follow the prayer, I took a sip of tea. *I've gotten two calls. One hung up. And the other one was my boss. How dare Stanley ask me to take out the trash on my show. He put the old coffee grounds in the can, where they'll stay. And if it stinks, it stinks.*

I whined, "Life stinks. People die in tragic accidents. And I'm the one held accountable for the trash?"

Then, like a nudge from God, I knew I'd take out the trash. Like always, God's whisper of love came to me, a reminder to cast my cares on Him. He also reminded me to be respectful of my elders, too—like Stanley.

I can forget to be a good example even though I want everyone else to be one. I mumble and grumble like the wandering Israelites. The Lord is great at showing me how He's the guide for my steps, the correction for my attitude, and the light for my walk.

I sighed, unable to fathom not coming to the radio station. But are my talk show days over? Stanley's right, no one is listening. And with Hudson moving in behind me, it may be time to move out of town and find a fresh start for good.

The commercial ended, and I read a verse about being anxious for nothing. Yet, inside, my heart pounded, and I felt all the blood in my heart gathering in my leg, ready to explode.

Then I announced, putting on my work face and using my professional voice, "Well, it's late on Tuesday night. We have fifteen minutes left, and you're telling me that no one out there has a question? I mean, could I be the only person who deals with the voices of her past? Am I the only person awake tonight? Let me ask you, listeners. Do you ever feel like God is a distant God, hiding behind the stars in the sky? As if He's throwing things at you in the dust of the night?"

The phone line lit up, and I shook with excitement. "Hello, yes. This is Beth Bender, with KNBO. Who do I have the pleasure of speaking to?"

The caller hung up. And my heart stopped mid-beat. "Well, folks. I guess that was the wrong number again." The phone lit up as I finished my sentence. I pushed the button. "Yes, this Beth Bender. Your friend. And your neighbor at KNBO."

The voice growled, "What kind of neighbor does what you did?" *Click.*

I cleared my throat. "Listeners, I'm not sure who called, but I do wish he'd call back. I'm not sure what to make of what he said." My stomach gurgled, my nerves were tingling under my skin, and I was pretty sure I knew the voice.

The phone blinked as another call came in. "Hello, this is Beth …"

The caller interrupted me. "Who was that? What did that man mean?"

"Stanley? Get off the phone. I'm trying to host a talk show." I realized we were *live* as I scolded my best friend and mentor. "Well, folks, my boss is worried I'm in danger. Will someone call him and tell him a bedtime story? He's having trouble going to sleep."

Stanley ignored my sarcasm. "I'm on my way. You shouldn't be there alone. I'll pick you up early."

"Stanley. Stop talking. My show's almost over. You're on the air.

Click.

Before I could share a story or comment, two calls came in simultaneously. "Callers, we're on a roll. Let me see who is on the first line." I pressed the blinking light. "Hello, this is Beth Bender. Your host at KNBO. It's Tuesday night. Talk to me."

The woman's voice warned me. "Don't hang up. He's on his way. Keep talking to me. I've called the police. So, tell me when they get there. So, I'll know you're safe."

I coughed. "And who am I talking to?"

"Never mind. Your doors are locked, right?"

"Excuse me, ma'am. Do I know you?"

"No, well, maybe. Just keep talking until the patrol car arrives. My husband's pretty upset."

"Let me put you on hold. The other line is ringing."

I pressed line two. "Hello, this is Beth Bender. Tell me. What's on your heart?"

"How dare you? After all these years, you've gotten away with it. Then you play with my son. He said that you let him come inside your house today. You've crossed the line."

I choked, doing my best not to hang up. "Sir, let me get this straight. So, we're neighbors?"

The man growled, "Don't act like you don't know me."

"Then tell the listeners who you are. They might want to take part in our conversation."

"Stop toying with me. You are not allowed to speak to my son again. And he's not allowed to speak to you. I'm sure he'll forget what I told him because he thinks you're nice. But I know the real you. It's time for this town to know what you did. Why don't you tell them?"

I sighed, "I'm sorry I've upset you. I have a verse for you. It's found in Psalm 121 and speaks about knowing that our help comes from the Lord."

The voice cut me off. "Stop with the scriptures. Your verses won't change what happened."

My heart pounded outside my chest, and the not-so-nice words that I longed to unload into the mic landed on the floor, and I kicked them around with my feet. "Stop accusing me. You can't do this on my show."

"I can do whatever I want. Besides, I'm on my way up there. You've gotten away with this for too long! You're going to face me, once and for all."

"Excuse me, so are you threatening me?"

"Call it what you will."

"You can't harass me like this."

"It seems like I'm doing a pretty good job of it."

I pressed the hold button down, went back to the other line, but the woman caller had hung up. I set the radio station to recorded worship songs and darted from the booth to the front foyer, making sure Stanley had locked the door.

There was a shadow outside, but thankfully, it was Stanley fumbling with the keys on the other side, and I waved for him to hurry. Realizing I had access to the twisty knob, I turned it. The sweat on my brow ran into my eyes like fear escaping my past as it crashed into my present.

Stanley bounced inside, locking the door. He wiped his forehead, grappling for what to say to me. "Beth, what was that about? Do you know who called?"

"Which one? There were two calls after your call to take out the trash."

"Why was that man calling you and saying you know what you did? Was that Hudson Hinkle? And the woman tried to warn you. Who was that? And why now, what's going on?"

I shook, shivering with the truth I held deep within. "It was Hudson. I'm positive. He came by here earlier to scream at me when you were on the air. He … has moved into his old house behind me! Can you believe that? And I think the woman who tried to warn me was Mindy, his wife."

"You know Hudson's wife?"

"No, not really. Somehow, I know her name, though."

Stanley ushered me to the back of the building. "Well, I've called the police too. He made threats. You could be in danger. We must put a stop to this."

I countered him. "Maybe his past was extra loud tonight. Tomorrow, he'll have a better perspective. We all say things we shouldn't."

"No, I've already called the police. They're sending a patrol car out here to make sure we get home without an incident. Mindy was worried about you, too."

"Stanley, don't panic. Hudson's angry. He won't hurt me. He's in a tough spot."

"How many years will he remain in that spot and keep you reeled in like a fish on the hook of his sorrow? We're not letting him hurt you. Or do something he'll regret."

From down the hallway, flashing lights flickered outside. We moved to the parking lot and spent a few minutes giving the officer our statements. I urged the policeman. "Now, don't arrest him. Hudson's harmless. He hasn't liked me for years. Please, just let him cool off."

The sleepy-eyed officer asked, "Are you sure we don't need to make a stop at his house?"

"He never showed up. I don't want to press charges. No harm done here tonight." I rubbed my leg, the ache of the wound deeper than I first thought.

Stanley nudged me. "I'll stay with her tonight. She doesn't need to be alone."

I rolled my eyes. "Stanley, you're eighty. You can't protect me." I giggled, making light of the situation.

"Seriously, I'm staying. And that's final. Oh, by the way, I won't be eighty until November."

As Stanley parked his pickup next to my car in the driveway, I jumped from my seat and hobbled to the front door, pulling out my keys from my satchel.

I opened the screen, and the door creaked, swinging away from me. I froze for a minute, unsure what to make of my unlocked door.

BEAUTY IN THE DARK

I rushed back to the truck. "Stanley, hurry. Someone's broken into the house. The front door is wide open."

He yawned a coyote howl, stepping from his truck. "Good, let's get some sleep."

"No, listen to me. The deadbolts weren't locked, and the door was partially open. When you picked me up for work, I remember locking the door. I'm sure of it."

Stanley pulled on my arm. "So, let's get back into my truck. Where's your cell phone? We need to make another call and have the police go inside before we do, in case someone broke into your home."

I twirled around in the yard, shadows everywhere dancing with movement. Maybe it was nothing or something. The night was silent except for our conversation. I waited as if the shadows might speak. As if the darkness might swallow us whole.

I climbed into the cab. "What in the world? This can't be happening to me." I dialed the phone. "Yes, this is Beth Bender again. No, no problem at the radio station. I'm at home. It appears someone has broken into my house."

The dispatcher asked, "Does it look like forced entry? Any broken glass?"

"Well, no. The front door is open, though."

"I'll send a patrol car. We had another call about a break-in just a few blocks from you. Don't go inside."

"Yes, ma'am." I tapped the button to end the call and turned to Stanley, whose head rested on the steering wheel, his fingers wrapped around it. I nudged him. "Some bodyguard you are."

He flopped to the left, bumping his jaw on the window. "Gladys, stop pushing me. I'm not snoring."

"Stanley, wake up. You're not at home. We're in your truck at my house."

He mumbled, almost like he'd forgotten we were sitting in the dark. "Where are we? Oh yeah, are the police coming? We must be wearing them out tonight." He ran his hand through his thinning hair. "Did I fall asleep? That's right; I can't be tired. It's only the middle of the night."

"Stop joking. This is serious. I didn't tell you this earlier, but when you saw me by my house earlier, I said goodbye to Colt, who is Hudson's son. But I didn't know it at that moment. Colt is in my children's choir at church, too. And now, as you do know, Hudson's banned Colt from having anything to do with me. He threw the sheet music at me."

I heard a voice inside saying the biggest and bravest thing to my soul. *Your life is precious. Moments hurt. Things cut at you. Remembering bad things won't make things better. You need to sing again. Life cuts both ways. Don't waste today.*

Stanley put his hand up, waving his arm in front of my face. "Sheet music? So now you're scared of sheet music? Now that does seem scary if you ask me."

"Stop it. This is not a good time to play with my emotions. It's not the sheet music I'm afraid of. It's that Hudson is convinced the accident was my fault. Earlier, I gave little Colt his paper, and he followed me into the house carrying Beauty. Goodness, I had no idea he was Hudson's son. Hudson is back and taunting me. And he's broken into my house!"

Stanley wiped his eyes with both hands. "I knew that it was Hudson in the white car when we left for work, but I didn't want to say a thing. You've been out of sorts, and that wasn't going to help."

I shook my head. "When were you going to tell me?" I crossed my arms like a scared twenty-year-old from my past.

"Calm down. He just moved across town to another house. He's been here a while, so something's triggered him. He hasn't bothered you in person before now, so we'll figure this out."

"Figure this out? I've put up with emails every year. He's stuck in the past."

Stanley put up his hand like a stop sign. "You're stuck, too. You have more locks on one door than I have on both doors at home. You have your windows bolted down, too. You have cameras outside to monitor for trespassers. Yet, you're worried at every turn."

I clapped my hands. "That's it. Cameras! I have the intruder on camera. I can look it up on the app on my phone. I grabbed my cell, tapped the screen, and scrolled for the app, tapping and looking until I found movement in the reel. "Wait, look, there's someone. Wait, he's gone to the porch from the side of the street. I can't see his face."

Stanley countered my assessment and glanced at the replay again. "That's you a few minutes ago. You were about to unlock the door when you saw it swing open."

"He had a hoodie on; that's not me."

"That's no hoodie; it's your long hair. It's dark out here, right? Besides, you forgot to turn on your porch light."

"I didn't forget the light. I never forget to turn it on."

"Never? Never say never."

I hit the loop on the history, going back in time on the recording. "But there's no one else. Not anyone, except ... except for Beauty. Look, she nudged the screen open and squeezed outside earlier tonight. Could the door have been open for hours?"

"Maybe you left the door unlocked. You were quite agitated today."

Ka-plunk.

Startled, I jumped in my seat, focusing on the hood of the truck. "Beauty, what are you doing? Look, Stanley, it's my kitty. She didn't run off."

"As I said, I'm sure you left the door open and didn't pull it closed. Beauty slips outside when she can; she's a roamer who doesn't get many chances since you keep her inside most of the time."

"She is an old cat. With these younger strays, she's afraid of them. And those three dogs across the street, they'll chase her."

I got out of the truck and picked Beauty up from the hood. She cradled in my arms as I sat back down, locking the door. "Where is that patrol car?"

"No need to lock the pickup. We're safe. It was you in the video. And it's obvious, you left the door open." Stanley turned, glancing over his shoulder. "I see a car's headlights. I'm sure that's the police."

The patrol car slowed, turned, and parked behind my car and Stanley's truck. I held Beauty and marched to the officer who got out of the passenger side, while Stanley met the one on the driver's side. He whispered, but I knew Hudson was telling the officer he was sure my forgetfulness played into the open-door saga.

The officer moved across the yard. "We'll go in first. We'll search the house and make sure it's safe."

Stanley and I leaned on the patrol car, and Beauty wiggled in my arms, ready to follow the officers. "No, girl. Let's make sure the inside of the house doesn't have any intruders."

From the corner of the yard, I saw a flash of light. "Is that you, Officer?" I scooted sideways like someone going stage right on a show where the actors move on and off to let the storyline move ahead. "Wait? Who is that? No! It's you! Hudson?"

The flashlight blinded me. "It's not what you think. I saw lights and a commotion. I came to see if you were all right."

"What? It's not like you care if I'm alive, let alone all right! As for lights, we sat in the dark. The only light was from the patrol car. Why were you standing in your driveway this late? It's the middle of the night." I drilled Hudson as if I had the right to question him.

"I don't sleep at night. I have insomnia. I was putting the trash can on the street when the police car came up."

"What? It sounds like you made that up." I knocked the flashlight to the ground, and Hudson picked it up.

I shouted, "Get off my property. You came to my work tonight and threw your son's sheet music down. You also called me on my talk show. Who does that? And your wife called to warn me. Please leave me alone. You've got to stop with the annual emails, too." I stomped forward with each command, pointing my finger at Hudson.

Then my sleepy-eyed boss placed himself between us.

I shouted, "Stanley, I can handle this."

"I'm not worried about that, but it's been a long day." Stanley waved for Hudson to leave.

Hudson sighed. "I'm upset, not so much at you, but how this house took me back in time. I didn't know I'd get so mad or lose my temper. But when Colt told me you were his choir director and that he'd come over to your house and come inside, I lost it. Fortunately, I didn't yell at him, but after he went to bed tonight, Mindy, that's my wife, we argued over whether we should have moved here or not."

I put my cat down, so I could talk with both arms. "Don't waste your breath on trying to explain anything to me. I've had it with you. You can't blame me anymore. I never had any part in the accident. You don't know what happened before my husband left that day. And besides, I don't owe you any explanation. It was horrible for you. And for me."

From my left, the two officers rushed to the side of the yard, where my full-blown anger released years of unresolved pain, and I exploded like a volcano of harsh words. One officer touched my shoulder. "The house is clear. Nothing seems to be missing. We checked the closets and under your bed. Let's take this inside."

The other officer hovered near Hudson. "And you, sir, there's nothing to see here. I suggest you go home."

Hudson nodded, his flashlight casting a beam that sent Beauty chasing it across the grass. "I live behind Ms. Beth. I'll call it a night."

Stanley let out his goodbye remark. "Hudson, keep your distance. And watch what you say on my radio station. I protect those I love. And Beth is like my own daughter."

Hudson slid to the street, walking by my wooden fence, the one that can't keep out the past or the new neighbors. I counted his steps, as if it mattered, and when he got to the back of my yard, he had to step around the giant green trash can by the corner of the driveway.

My anxiety shot to the sky like an invisible rocket; the ability to stand and speak to Hudson with force was not something I planned. I usually cower from disagreements, except for banter and sarcasm with friends. But tonight, I found a strength that surged within me, like confidence and assurance. And I stood my ground, even if I sounded a little hateful.

After I apologized for two phone calls for police assistance and changed into my sweats, Stanley sat on my couch, nodding off with his chin on his chest. Beauty curled up in his lap, and I plopped down beside them, yawning. "I'm worn out. I'm going to bed."

Stanley exhaled, his chest rising, and the whistle from his nostrils caused Beauty to cut her eyes at him. His inhale lasted for a minute longer than most should. He sighed, "Sorry, as I get older, I smack more often with my new teeth, my nose whistles without asking me, and my stomach makes awful noises."

I petted Beauty, and her purring was a sign she was ready for sleep, too. I leaned on Stanley's shoulder. "I've got to get some rest, too. Did you lock the front door?"

Without answering me, Stanley took out his false teeth, dropping them in the small bowl of water on the end table. "They need to breathe."

I grimaced. "Did you have to do that with me sitting here? And can't you put them in the bathroom or somewhere out of sight?"

"They go where I go. I paid good money for those teeth."

I marched to the front of the living room. "And by the way, I asked, did you lock the front door?"

Stanley wiped his bumpy nose. "Yes, I locked the door. I made sure. And where is that pillow you promised?"

"Oh, yeah. I'll be right back. I'll get you a blanket too. I like the cool air when I sleep. I turn the air conditioning to around 68 degrees. You'll need covers."

In my room, I took a pillow from my bed, retrieved a blanket from the closet shelf, and knocked an old shoebox to the floor. I shoved all the items back inside the box, not wanting to see one thing that was inside—since the past lurked beneath the lid.

I placed the box on the shelf and rushed to an already sleeping Stanley, bent in half, ready to fall forward. "You're going to land on the floor." I tapped his shoulder. "Swing up your feet. I'll cover you up."

"I'm awake. Gladys, did I miss the end of the show? Wait, where's Gladys?"

"She is at home. You're at my house. You called her an hour ago. She knows you're making me a prisoner in my own home."

"I'm protecting you. Simple, good ole friendship in action."

I squealed a yawn that released like a call to the wild. "Sorry, I'm exhausted. And don't wake me up in the morning. It's pushing two. If you get up before I do, let yourself out."

"I can find my way to my truck. I'll call and see if we can get your car in the shop, too."

"Thank you, Stanley. I mean it. You're the mentor everyone could use — annoying at times — but you never give up on people. You came alongside me when I was hurting and afraid to live. I'll never forget how you and Gladys loved me through the storm of my horrible sorrow."

Stanley patted my head as I covered him with the blanket. "We need sleep or we'll both sound like robots on the radio tomorrow."

"Yes, we do. Good night, Captain." I put the pillow beneath Stanley's head, and he tugged on the blanket, tucking it under his chin. "It's freezing in here."

"I told you I like a cool house."

"Like I said, it's freezing." Beauty wrapped herself into a ball at Stanley's feet.

I kissed Beauty on the head, inhaling a whiff of ruined eggs that were obviously left in the sun, and realized it was Stanley's socks. Although they were sour, the socks were inviting to my cat. "Night, sweet kitty. At least you can keep his toes warm."

I checked the doors one more time. All locked. I went to my bedroom, ready to collapse into my bed. I pulled the comforter back, fluffed my pillow, but I was distracted by the sound of water dripping, more like splashing. I crawled over the bed, peeked out the blinds, and the running water was louder, like a small gushing river outside in the backyard.

At the back door, I unlocked it and peeked outside. "What? The sprinkler is running?"

Turning the knob, my feet splashed in the pool of water which had flooded the grass, and I glanced around the yard, the streetlight on the far corner by my fence casting shadows, but I could see that I was alone.

Stanley stuck his head through the door, looking at me. "What are you doing? I was asleep. Now I'm up. What is your problem?"

"Someone turned on my water and left it running." I held out my hands as if directing traffic. "This is not a good sign. Someone has been here."

"Weren't you watering your yard earlier when I came to pick you up for work?"

"I was. But that sprinkler was hooked to the hose on another faucet, located to the side of the house. I turned it off when Colt left. But …"

Stanley slurred his words, his lips in need of teeth. "You don't remember if you came back here to turn this one off?"

"You're right. I don't remember." I cried. "Stanley, it's happening again. I'm falling apart."

"You're exhausted. That's all."

"No, I'm falling apart. Last time, I ended up in the hospital. My emotions are taking over again."

"Come inside. Let me make sure you fall asleep before I do. I'll read your favorite passage to you. You always said my voice puts you to sleep, which makes me wonder how many sermons you've slept through when I was your pastor."

I smiled. "Stanley, I've got to get a handle on things." I exhaled, wiped my feet on the patio rug, and rushed to my bedroom, where I fell onto the mattress and pulled up the covers.

Stanley sat across the room, his lips flapping as he read to me from my Bible, words about having courage and not being afraid. I closed my eyes, snuggling with my pillow. I peeked with one eye. "Get some sleep, Stanley. We need rest."

He flipped the light switch, the padding sound of his sock feet fading down the hallway. I could count sheep, blue, red, and purple ones. I got to thirty-five and opened my eyes. I was still awake.

Then, Stanley corrected my cat with a mousey tone. "Not right now, girl. Sleep. We need sleep before I collapse."

I sat up, unsure whether to see what Beauty was up to or go to sleep. I moved from the bed, unable to mind my own business, and I glanced down the hallway, not hearing anything. "Stanley. Are you awake?"

Nothing. Not a sound, except for my loudmouth.

I inched to the living room to check on Beauty and Stanley, confident I was going to wake him up one more time. He's getting too old to keep up with me, although he'd argue the point.

I entered the living room; they were gone, so I turned toward the kitchen, where the back door was cracked open.

I called Stanley as I slid across the tile toward the light switch. "Stanley?"

That's when my foot hit a lump and I heard a moan coming from the floor. "Stanley?"

I knelt beside him; the blood pooled on the slate tile beside his head. "What happened? Let me get help!"

OOZING WITH BLOOD

I stirred awake after sitting, sleeping, wiggling, and waiting. No one should have to sit in the hospital parking lot because of the one-visitor rule. And with Stanley in intensive care, and Gladys at his side, I'm stuck out in his pickup. Last night, I almost forgot to wake up Gladys to alert her. Finally, I found Stanley's keys by his teeth, and then I drove and picked her up.

I dug into my pockets, groggy from a few hours of sleep in the truck, and twitched and wiggled while waiting for news about Stanley. "Nice, just what I needed, his dentures! Wait, maybe a set of teeth could get me inside Stanley's room—at least for a few seconds. He'll want them."

I pulled the face mask from my pocket and tossed the dentures into the other pocket, where they clinked together as if Stanley spoke from his upper and lower plates, reminding me to cover for him at the radio station. "Stanley, I'll go in around four. Reed has us covered."

I imagined his teeth clanked with another answer; one I ignored.

Inside the double doors of the hospital lobby, I stood by the elevator, ready to find Stanley. My reflection in the silver door showed wild hair in need of a brush. I smoothed my hair with finger-brushing and straightened my shirt, noticing the blood oozing through the fabric of my sweatpants. "This isn't better. I will need more bandages."

The elevator door opened, and two men stormed by me, their conversation tense, inaudible. I got into the box and pushed the second-floor button, sighing deeply. The closed-in elevator made me panic, sweat, and caused my feet to tingle. The door opened, and I let out a yell. "I can breathe now. I can breathe. I hate riding in elevators!"

The four ladies approaching grimaced, their faces doused with question marks, and they frowned. They went out of their way to go around me. The one with outdated curls whispered, "Is she a patient that's gotten loose? Do they have a psychiatric ward here?"

I held the elevator door open for them. "I'm not a patient. I'm tired. I'm being followed and harassed by my new neighbor. My talk show is probably going to be canceled. They'll sell the radio station, and I'll be without a job. Do you hear me? I will be all alone again!"

The woman to my left with giant hands slipped my fingers off the door. "We're in a hurry. Did you know your leg is bleeding?"

I glanced down, my white tennis shoe on my right leg, red with color, damp with blood. "I need Band-Aids. That's all," I hollered. "I don't need a psychiatric ward. I promise. I need to find Stanley."

With that, the elevator door shut, the ladies trapped inside, and I was free. Well, until the security guard showed up and asked, "Ma'am, can I help you? Do you need to see a doctor?"

I yanked the false teeth from my pocket. "No! I need to give Stanley his teeth. He's in a room somewhere. I don't know which floor or where the intensive care unit is. I hoped this was the right place."

The guard came to my side. "You seem a little uneasy."

"I'm not unstable. I get nervous in elevators. And I had a little panic attack."

"But your leg is bleeding. Let's take you down to the emergency room. Do you have your identification with you?"

"Fine, I just need a bandage. Then will you tell me where to find Stanley?"

"Sure thing. Come with me. We'll take the stairs since you're not happy with the elevator."

"Wait, don't make fun of me. I'm fine. And get your hands off my shoulder. I'm not in the mood." My words shouted with a tone of the old person responding to abuse behind closed doors from long ago.

The absence of light escaped me, and my eyes rolled backwards. "I'm dizzy. Wait, maybe I need help. I cut my leg last night. I've changed out the bandage three times. When I got out of the truck and came inside, I think I scraped it on the door and broke the wound open."

The guard motioned for me to follow. "Let's go this way. Just come with me. Please."

I wobbled, collapsing, weak from the stress and having had little sleep. The guard cradled me in his arms. "Let me help you. We all need help sometimes."

I whimpered and rambled, "I remember a summer's day. I remember the sprinkler. The laughter. The way I sipped on mango tea. I remember the last hour. The sour. The way time stopped. The moment when he took his last breath in this hospital."

The guard holding me inhaled, his chest rising and falling. "You'll be fine. We're going to help you."

I placed my head against his shoulder. "I'm tired. I'm frustrated. I'm holding my breath. I'm worn out. I'm lost. I'm hurting. I can't change the past. I don't know how to do this. My desert life is a blister of burns ..."

I felt myself go limp, my legs bouncing with each step the man took, and he carried me like a father might cradle his child.

On the skinny bed in the emergency room, I clenched my lips together like a small girl, unable to fathom how my walk with dentures became a useless trip that took me to where doctors and nurses whispered and prodded and analyzed my behavior.

I prayed, "Lord, take me from this desert place. Your love for me doesn't change. Lord, lead the way. Your relentless grace is for me. Draw me closer. Please show me a better way. Carry me beyond the closed-off places that suffocate me."

A nurse stepped back into the room. "We're going to stitch up your leg." She cleaned, wiped, used an ointment, and wiped some more. "I've found your Pastor Stanley and his wife, Gladys. They're in room 236."

I perked up. "See, I really was looking for someone. That doctor didn't believe me. He thought I was on drugs or something."

She continued her work on my shin. "His job was to consider your health and what the problem was that caused your breakdown."

"Breakdown? I'm tired. That's all. It's been rough these past few days. The last time I went to a hospital was when my husband ... my husband died."

"What happened?" The nurse created a design like she loved crocheting skin together.

I sighed, "My husband used to hit me. It was twenty years ago, but lately, it feels like yesterday." The words escaped like blood trickling from my mouth. "I usually don't talk about it. It was horrible. Rhett used to lock me in the bathroom when he drank too much and leave me in there for hours; then he would come in and drag me to the bathtub. He would call me trash and tell me no one could love a person like me. He would turn on the hot water, not much cold, and scorch my skin, saying I was dirty and needed cleansing. He'd threaten to kill me."

The nurse wiped her face as a tear fell. "I'm so sorry he treated you like that."

I covered my eyes. I couldn't believe I'd shared the deepest part of me with a stranger.

The nurse sniffled, her brown eyes filled with tears, and she stopped stitching, snipping the thread. "There you are. Your leg has about eighteen stitches. You could have gotten a nasty infection from that wound." She rolled her stool up toward my head. "I'm sorry you had to go through that with your husband. Life gets so hard, and we get caught being trapped by those chapters. There's no reason you should ever be a punching bag for someone else."

"I didn't know how to find my way out of it, back then. I was afraid to leave. And afraid to stay. He scared me so. And I was a prisoner at his beck and call."

She nodded. "My daddy did things like that to my mother. She never left him and hid it as best she could. It's a miracle she could ever breathe. People thought my dad was the most upstanding man. He had his own accounting business and took part in community activities, but at home, he was a bombshell. He died when I was in high school, and my mother never married again. But she smiles now. She plants flowers. And sews."

I smiled. "You apparently sew too." I pointed to my leg.

"Yes, I decided to become a nurse to help people. Saving lives is fulfilling, too. It gives me purpose."

I realized I'd reached for her hand, and she held it tightly. I wiped my nose with the back of my other hand. "Thank you for listening. And thank you for fixing my leg. You've helped me to remember that I need to breathe, and that I should let go of those pieces from my past that keep locking me in the elevator of life."

The nurse smiled. "I'll be right back. I'll see what I can do to make sure you get to go home. I'm sure you'll heal better in your own bed."

I nodded. "I need a Kleenex, too."

"Sure thing. I'll be back in a few minutes."

**

I stared at the ceiling, the ache in my leg stinging some, but at least the oozing had stopped. From the doorway, I heard a song, a familiar hymn, coming closer. The singer was none other than Gladys, who sings like a cardinal wishing to become a blue jay with a crow's voice. "Amazing grace, how sweet the sound, that saved a wretch like me. I once was lost, but now I'm found. I was blind, but now I see."

I called with a weak whisper of exhaustion. "Gladys? Keep walking, I'm here. Come to my room. Don't stop. Or I'll have to get up and come get you."

Within seconds, which felt like four hundred hours, a round, gray-haired woman with glasses peeked into my room. "Well, what do we have here? And what happened to your leg?"

"It's a long story, but how is Stanley? Is he awake? Is he talking? What do you know?"

She wiggled the silver stool, and it wobbled. "I was going to sit on that, but I'd be in the hospital next." She giggled, her laughter salve to my heart. "Stanley's awake. He has a cut and about ten stitches. He's giving orders for me to get to the station to help Reed. He'll be fine—if his headache lets up."

I shook my head. "I don't know what happened. I'd gotten into bed. And after a bit, I heard him scolding Beauty. Then I found him on the floor, and for some reason, the back door was wide open."

"Well, Stanley knows he needs to wear his glasses. He can't see very well. And it turns out, he got turned around going to the bathroom and tripped over Beauty. He got mad at her because she wanted to go outside and kept meowing. So, he opened the back door and slipped on his socks. He was prepared to leave her outside for the rest of the night."

"No way! His stinky socks caused him to fall?"

"Yes. He's simply getting older. Sometimes we stumble over our feet at our age. A little bit ago, I decided it's time for us to slow down and follow through on selling the radio station. You can see if you can make it profitable and keep KNBO on the air. But if you don't buy it, we'll put the place on the market. Stanley and I, we're closer to heaven than most folks."

I snapped, "Don't say that. You have a lot of good years left."

"Well, let's just say we're closer to Jesus in many ways." She patted my arm. "The doctor is keeping Stanley one more day for observation. But he'll be fine."

"Can I see him? I just came inside the hospital to bring his teeth, and things blurred and closed in around me. The loss of blood from my leg didn't help either."

"Well, he's resting. But not to worry, Stanley will be home tomorrow, Lord willing. I'm staying with him tonight, but could you bring me a few items from the house? The key is under the planter by the back door."

"Sure, I'll be out of here soon. Just tell me what you need, and I'll pick it up. If you don't mind, I'll drive Stanley's truck today and tomorrow. My car isn't cooperating."

Gladys hummed, found a pen in her purse, and an old receipt. "I'll write down a few things for you. Oh, where are Stanley's teeth?"

"In the pocket of my hoodie."

She moved across the room, and for the first time, I noticed how much slower Gladys walked, yet still gracefully. She turned back to me. "I want to say, thank you. I'll always be grateful that you couldn't go to sleep without being nosy. Because of you, Stanley got to the hospital and didn't have to sleep on the kitchen floor." Gladys giggled under her breath, giving me a wink.

After Gladys left, I hobbled over to my jeans, tossing off the ugly caped robe the hospital had provided. "They need to put a sunflower print on these things. They're awful." Dressed, I peeked up and down the hall, my leg aching, but thankfully, not bleeding. I hoped for the nurse and watched for a doctor. I called the person in the white shirt at the end of the hallway. "Do you know if I can leave? I'm supposed to go home."

I leaned on the doorframe, waiting for someone to come back. The man motioned he'd get someone, but patience isn't my best virtue.

I grabbed the truck keys, slipped on my hoodie, and limped to the exit, pushing the red button on the wall, and then someone called me. "Ms. Bender? We need to talk. Your discharge papers aren't ready."

I waved to the doctor. "I'm discharged. Please send me a bill. You have my address. And tell the nurse, I'll never forget her. She's the best!"

The doors closed behind me, and I rushed outside, through the emergency exit, under the awning. An ambulance rolled in beside me, and I muttered, "Thank goodness, they didn't admit me or put me in the psych ward. Once was enough. Even if it was just two days. The trauma of Rhett's accident put me there, along with the secrets of dealing with the physical and emotional abuse. I'd lost myself back then and my way. But not now, I'm free. And from now on, I'm taking the stairs. No more elevators for me."

In the parking lot, the same guard from the second floor rode up on a security golf cart. "Excuse me, it seems you've forgotten to take care of a few things back in the emergency room."

I shook my head. "I'll be fine. If you've ever given someone the benefit of the doubt, please, let it be with me. And let it be today."

"I'm doing my job. I can't let you leave."

"But I've got pressing things to do. I've got to stay out of the elevator of my past. Haven't you ever had a bad day?"

Mr. Guard put his hands on the steering wheel. "Go on. Before I change my mind."

"Thank you. Tell them to send me the bill. And that nurse, tell her she's a blessing! Oh, wait, so are you!"

I charged off, grimacing from the pull on my stitches while freedom waited for me at home.

Pam Kumpe

BACKYARD TEA

In my backyard, I sat at my small wrought iron table, where decorative metal ornaments—a bumblebee and a ladybug—sat. Next to the chair, off from the patio, four metal daisy flowers added color to the yard. And on the pecan tree, a metal woodpecker held onto the trunk, and a cardinal on a stake shot from the base of the tree. Near the fence, three sunflowers and more metal decorated the fencerow with yellow blooms.

The bird feeder was now full of seed, and the sprinkler spritzed the grass with a much-needed drink of water. A rainbow shot up when the spray came to my side of the yard, something I love to see—it never grows old.

Gladys was set for the night with Stanley, and I have about two hours before heading to the station. "Beauty, I hope you enjoyed your little excursion last night. You're not an outside cat. Don't forget it."

Meow. Meow.

I picked up my cell to complete my text message to my good friend, Sally. I wanted to send her updates on Stanley and the radio station, on Hudson and little Colt, and how we'd go shopping next week. I glanced down. She'd sent a heart and the words, I love you.

I sipped on my tea —cranberry orange this time —and enjoyed a reprieve in the shade, as the August sun wasn't so hot today. I was fresh from a shower, a blast of water that used just the right hot and cold, where shampoo burned my eyes, and where my soul refreshed itself. "Beauty, I think it's time for fresh paint and new tile in the bathroom. What do you think?"

She skirted around me like a Slinky, well, more like a soft and bendable toy. "I'm ready to get a new look in there. It's filled with too many ugly moments. We need to add some color, like sunflowers or daisies."

I held my tumbler and walked around the sprinkler, hoping my leg would ease up, the shooting pains fierce as nails. I heard myself say out loud, "So, Beth, who can you trust? Who is willing to help you stay out of the elevator of your past?"

The afternoon air, still and unmoving, sent me back to the shade, where I sat down, my leg taking on a heartbeat. I spoke to the ladybug and bumblebee. "Did you know the Bible says the heart is deceitful? And that means I can't always trust myself. I can't trust my thoughts either."

The ladybug and bumblebee didn't answer.

At the hospital, I lost control of the elevator, and the unresolved feelings of not saying goodbye to Rhett boxed me in. My ability to focus was overshadowed by my emotions, too. When Rhett died, I tucked away the grief, the secrets, and the sorrow. But the pain was just under the skin, ready to bleed on someone else.

I stood at the edge of the sprinkler, getting my toes wet. "It's becoming clearer each day that I cannot put my trust in anything except God. He's my solid foundation, without Him, I sink and fall and fumble and collapse with fear."

A small face peeked into the yard from the gate as the latch slipped up, and Colt stepped into the backyard. "Colt, what are you doing?"

"I heard you talking, and I peeked through the fence." He marched to the other chair on the patio, plopping down, his flip-flops dropping from his feet.

"Colt, I'm sorry, but I think you need to go home. Your daddy wants you home." I pointed to his house behind my fence.

"He's not home. Mommy's watching a movie. I was bored. Can I stay for a little while?"

"We don't want to disobey your daddy. He's not going to be happy if he finds out you came over here."

"But I was bored." He moved closer to the sprinkler, holding out his hand, ready to get soaked if given the encouragement.

"Colt, let me walk you home."

"Can I jump into the sprinkler fast? I'll dry off playing basketball in my driveway."

I sighed. "One jump. But hurry."

His excitement lasted for a minute as Mindy stuck her face inside the gate from the side of the yard. "Colt Hinkle, get yourself home. You know that you aren't allowed to leave the yard without permission. Remember?"

"Yes, ma'am." He ran for his flip-flops, picked them up, and ran out the gate.

I moved closer to Mindy, her brown hair swishing as she started to leave. I touched her shoulder. "Can we talk for a minute? I wanted to thank you for calling the radio station the other night."

Mindy inhaled, her shoulders rising, and she looked back at me. "Hudson's not a bad man. He's in a bad place, mentally.

He lost his job at the paper mill, and since he'd always owned this house, we had to move. We couldn't afford the rent at the other place. And my small check doesn't cover our bills. If I could get more hours, then that would help."

I smiled. "Where do you work?"

"It's a small radio station in Texarkana. I do the jingles. I record them, answer the phone, and pay bills. Whatever needs to be done, I'm that person."

I gulped. "I work at KNBO. Well, I guess you already know that I work there. Hey, I don't make much either. But my house is paid for, thanks to this community. When I lost my husband, my church family rallied around me and paid off my mortgage. I think that's what they did for Hudson's family, too. At least, I heard that at the beauty shop."

"Wow, that's great. I've heard this is a great town."

"I was brought up here. It's home for me. Small town stuff tends to get repeated too much, but then a new topic comes along, and folks move onto it." I laughed; it was almost like I was talking about myself.

"I let Colt ride the church bus, hoping Hudson and I could follow behind him one Sunday. But now Hudson knows you lead the children's choir. So, I'm not sure when Colt will be back, if at all."

"I'm sorry. I didn't mean to make him mad at me or dredge up the past. I know that when Rhett caused the accident, the toll on Hudson was horrendous. He was ten, after all."

"I met Hudson in college, and he never talked about his father until we were engaged, and he let me know how it happened. He's held a grudge against you. And for that, I'm sorry."

I stepped closer. "We might have an opening soon at the radio station here. The owners are close to retiring. It would save you from driving to Texarkana; the gas you'd save would help."

"Thank you. I'll keep that in mind." Mindy pulled the gate open. "Do you know why Hudson is so mad at you?"

"Yes, he thinks I pushed Rhett out the door that day."

"No, that's not all of it; there are many layers to his grief. Hudson and his father were supposed to sing at his old home church that night. They were planning a duet. It was the song, 'Amazing Grace.' And Hudson said you took that all away from him."

"That's the song Colt is learning. I had no idea." I wobbled, my leg squeezing like someone was sewing my heart back together. "The day of the wreck was after my husband hit me and choked me." I stuttered, "That's right, my … my husband abused me. The day he left was the last time he slammed me against the wall."

Mindy held her neck. "I'm so sorry. I've heard that you went through a hard marriage."

"It was a tough two years. The day Peter's car got hit by Rhett, Hudson was playing in my yard with the water sprinkler. So, I'm sure that's why he was so angry when he found out Colt knew me." I folded my arms. "I don't know how this is going to work out. I know it's hard for you, too. Colt is the cutest thing. You should be so proud of him. He has such a gift for music. A beautiful voice."

Mindy wiped her eyes. "He's special. We tried four times and lost three babies before we had Colt. His birthday is in March. He'll be eight. And he's a joy."

"I'm sorry for being in the way. But thankfully, the fence will help."

Mindy moved closer to me, taking my hand. "We will find a way to be friends. It's going to take time, though. Hudson needs a job. That would help take some pressure off."

I shut the gate as Mindy left, and I called her through the fence. "Welcome to our neighborhood. And please, try to find a way for Colt to come to church. He needs to sing."

"I'll see what I can do. No promises, though."

**

At the radio station, I parked Stanley's truck and hurried inside to relieve Reed. He came to the hallway after setting his pre-recorded material for the next thirty minutes, which was a teaching on Job by a local pastor.

Reed met me in the break room. "How's Stanley? What happened? How did he fall?"

I sat next to the same stinky coffee pot. "Do you and Stanley ever think of emptying the coffee grounds and rinsing the pot before it smells up the place?"

"Fine, I'll clean it. But how did Stanley fall?"

"He tripped over my cat. Yes, I said it. It's my fault." I caught myself taking the blame, something that comes easily to me. Something I've got to stop doing.

Reed noticed me shaking my head. "Stop beating yourself up. Cats get in the way. I've stumbled over my two strays many times."

"I know, Beauty was pestering him to go outside. He didn't turn on the light, and his socks slipped on the tile. The socks had a lot to do with it. He's going to be fine, though."

"I'm relieved. He's the rock of this place. He keeps saying we're closing shop."

I rubbed my nose. "Well, let's make some plans. I'm going to try to buy the station. They're retiring. And soon."

"So that means, I'd work for you?" Reed wrinkled his nose like he was sniffing for something.

"Yes, I guess it would."

"Then I'd like a raise. Do you know how much they pay me? It's not enough to live on that, for sure."

"You don't need the money. You're retired from the bank and have your retirement income, not counting the property you've invested in. You're trying to get to me, already." I nudged him, his bony arm in need of muscles.

"Sorry, Boss. It didn't hurt to try and get a raise." He laughed, rinsed out the coffee pot, and emptied the coffee grounds.

I ordered. "Now, take out the trash."

"I thought that was your job." Reed clapped his hands as if he'd made a joke, as if he meant it, and yes, he was right, I'm the trash gal.

The night went as planned — nothing special, just a few phone calls for the talk show — and the time moved along at an incredible pace. Less and less my leg ached, and Reed drove to the station at midnight to see me get into Stanley's truck, to follow me home, and to watch me go into my house.

I stood on the porch. "Night, Reed. See you tomorrow. I'll be there by four."

In the backyard once more, for a late-night moment when the heat left and the cool settled in, I sat with my metal critters in the shadows, the streetlight giving me enough light to sit without the porch light on.

I heard chatter, or something. Voices maybe. Maybe it's the squirrels holding a midnight planning session on eating the bird food from the feeder while I'm gone tomorrow.

I walked to the middle of the yard to determine which direction the noise came from. Then, I knew it was Mindy and

Hudson having a heated, purposeful discussion. Their loud whispers verged on an argument, like two giant squirrels fighting, and the tension grew with each of them raising their voice.

THE FENCE OF RESOLUTION

Hudson argued with Mindy, "What were you thinking? Colt told me you spent time with Beth this afternoon while I was gone."

"It wasn't planned. He hopped over to play in her sprinkler, and I went after him. I didn't plan to make friends. Beth is nice, though. Give her a chance."

I absorbed their words, inching closer to the oak, standing behind it, not that they could see me through the wooden fence.

"Hudson, you've got to get past this. It's hurting your relationship with me and your son. Colt needs you."

"That's right, he needs me. He needs you. He doesn't need Beth!"

"But she's his choir teacher at church. She told me how great he sings. Why would you take that away from him?"

For a few minutes, no one talked, and I hovered close, ready to eavesdrop and see what more they might say. Then Hudson blasted. "Fine! He can sing. At church. Just don't let him go over to her house."

"Hudson, thank you. This means the world to him and to me."

I burst into applause, my hand hitting the aluminum tumbler in my grasp, my nervous reaction unplanned in the late-night spying.

Hudson called, "Beth, is that you? What are you doing out here listening to us?"

"Excuse me, I was having tea. I just got off work and heard talking. It's midnight. I'm up late a lot."

"Apparently, you like to know our business, too."

I apologized. "How did I know you'd be in the driveway talking? Most people are asleep."

Mindy added, "Colt will be at church. I'll send him on the bus."

I smiled at the fence. "I'm thrilled. This is so exciting."

Hudson growled from the other side like an attack dog. "Don't think this makes us friends. But Colt does love to sing. And we'll make sure he does, despite how I feel about you."

I shouted like a woodpecker hitting its beak on a tree. "I'm so excited. This is the best news ever."

Hudson announced, "I'm going inside."

Mindy's face popped up as she stood on the bottom ledge of the fence. "I'm so excited. We always discuss our differences away from Colt, so we came out here. I never expected Hudson to say yes. We've argued all night about this. And I've prayed he would change his mind, but this was the fastest answer and turnaround ever."

I moved closer. "So, he's inside, right?"

"Yes, Hudson's in the house. But I have something to ask you. One of the ladies at church, well, I called to have you checked out before I let Colt join the choir. She told me you love children and you're reliable and trustworthy. Anyway, she said you have a song hiding within you that you used to sing specials. That everyone wishes you'd return to the platform and sing. So why don't you sing?"

"It's complicated. So, you called to check me out?"

Mindy nodded. "Of course, you don't know whom you can trust these days. Colt's our baby; his needs come first. And we, of course, want to protect him."

I swallowed my pride. "As for my singing, I stopped after the wreck. Except to teach children to sing."

"Maybe your song is tucked inside your pocket, and it's time to get it out."

"I don't know. I'll think about it." My defensive mode kicked in, the words itchy under my skin, ready to travel to my mouth. I'm good with offering advice, not taking it.

Mindy continued, "The lady who answered the phone at church said you have a gift. That your voice lights up the sanctuary, and you should sing for God."

"Wait, I still serve at church. You make it sound like I've evaporated into thin air." I looked behind me to ensure I was in my backyard, as I felt like I was in the courtroom of life being judged.

"You may serve, but don't you want to be used by God?"

I swallowed my ugly answer because I wouldn't say it out loud. Instead, I responded with, "He is using me."

"Yes, but there's more inside you, waiting to find a way to fly, like a butterfly."

"I think I'm still in a cocoon phase."

"What would you tell your listeners?" Mindy's words cut deep, as if she removed the mask of my pretenses and somehow knew the real me, the one lost and hiding behind the call to her heart from God—to make music and rejoice in the Lord, always.

"It's complicated."

"You say that a lot." Mindy added, "You should sing. Do it on purpose. That's what you tell your students. Colt told me how you encourage the children to find their voice for Jesus. That they should give Him their best, plus, you say the same thing on your talk show, too, we should do our very best and honor the Lord by using our gifts for Him."

"So, you're paying attention to my show? And now, you're using my words against me." I chuckled, happy about the revelation of having a listener, but unsettled that my words were not always my actions—behind the scenes.

Mindy piped in with, "I've learned about you at the beauty shop, too. I'm going in the morning. This mop needs some style, and I'm getting a good trim." She brushed her brown hair with her fingers. "Everyone listens to you; they just don't call in that much."

I sighed. "I wish people would call. Maybe I should move the show to an earlier time slot."

"That might help, but who knows?" Mindy rambled on. "Now that we've moved behind you, I'm sure the word will get out about Hudson's little incident on the radio, too."

I nodded. "News does travel fast here."

"So, I'm going to make sure they talk about your show instead. Then I'll encourage them to call you on the show. I love turning the tide of conversations to redirect folks toward more pleasant chatter. And by the way, you should tell your story on the air too."

"I don't have a story." I squinted, unsure how Mindy knew me better than I knew myself.

"Seriously, you could help so many others if they knew the truth about your past and the pain and what you went through. You're a survivor of domestic abuse, right?"

I sipped on my tea. "I'm a survivor because my husband died. That's all. I might not have gotten out of that marriage alive if he hadn't left that day and wrecked his truck."

Mindy hung onto the fence. "Then help someone else. Help another woman get free. And free you'll be."

"I don't know. I just don't know." My breathing sped up, and my chest felt heavy with the reality of how the past weighs on me.

Mindy spoke with a crack in her voice, pausing for a moment. "I need your prayers, too. Hudson has severe anxiety about his health deteriorating. That's why he's edgy. He missed so much work; they had no choice but to let him go."

"What? He's sick?" My compassion rose from within, not that I expected to care about Hudson, but the calloused heart can often hide a kinder side, which I know so well.

"He's had juvenile diabetes since high school, takes insulin shots, has lost sight in one eye, and has kidney disease, plus a rare genetic disease, and even anemia, and takes hemoglobin injections. He's beginning dialysis soon, and we're planning on doing it here at the house. He'll have to do it for eight hours each night."

"Oh, Mindy. But he's only thirty!" My tears dripped like a broken water sprinkler.

She wept too. "It's been hard. Hudson's on the transplant list at Baylor Scott & White in Dallas, but who knows when that will happen."

"So, he could get a kidney?"

"He must get a pancreas and a kidney because a new kidney would be destroyed unless he received a pancreas. So, he must receive both at the same time. Our Colt was diagnosed with juvenile diabetes last August when he was six and ended up at the Children's Hospital in Little Rock. Hudson was devastated that he passed on the disease. We never saw that coming, so to say we're stressed and sad and anxious is an understatement."

"Mindy, I'm sorry. This must be hard on you, too."

"It is, but thankfully, Colt understands how to adjust his insulin with his pump. I thought his going to church would be a good start to a normal outing. I track his blood sugar levels on his Dexcom, which is on his arm, and on my phone too. I should have gone with him to church, but Hudson's struggling with his faith."

"I'll pray for your family. We never know what tomorrow brings, let alone our next breath. Our bodies break down without asking us, don't they?"

"Yes, and so do marriages. I hope mine survives this season. Mindy sobbed, "I should go in; it's late. I'm keeping you up. As for Hudson, his moods go up and down like a light switch. He could change his mind tomorrow and forget that he agreed to Colt going to church again. So yes, pray for me. And pray for Colt and Hudson."

I touched her fingers gripping the fence, and my empty tumbler dropped to the grass. "If you need to talk, come over anytime. I'm home in the daytime and usually go into the station at five in the evening, well, a little earlier this week with Stanley out of pocket."

"I work from six in the morning until two in the afternoon. Since he's out of school for the summer, Colt goes with me, plays games on my iPad, and helps me push buttons at the radio station. He's a whiz with computers."

I nodded. "I can't believe we both work at radio stations. We'll have a lot to talk about, but I do need some sleep." I yawned, my eyes weary and my mind in overload.

"Goodnight, it's nice to talk to someone. You're a friendly face in the dark and the light." Mindy disappeared behind the fence, her door clicking behind her, and the echo of my heart was thumping, the only sound I could now hear.

I picked up my tumbler, the moon lighting my way to the house, and I scooted across the grass toward the door, turning the sprinkler off. Beauty meowed, her soft cry a sorrowful tone as if she wept with Mindy. Could a cat know the heartache and pain escaping from a mother's heart and into my life? "Beauty, let's go to bed. We're never going to get up in the morning."

Inside, I climbed under the covers, and the mattress wrapped itself around me. Beauty pounced onto the bed, and she twirled in circles, making her nest at my feet.

I closed my eyes, and my thoughts soared, and I found myself saying out loud, "When I'm old and gray, let it be known that no one ever cared for me like Jesus. My treasure is in heaven, and if I should tell my story to help other women who suffer at the hands of abuse, let me be that voice. Let me speak the truth. And not hide behind the fence of my past anymore."

I tugged on my pillow, tossing, unsure where that declaration of purpose came from, yet knowing God has a way of getting my attention when I least expect it. I yawned for what seemed like hours, closing my eyes with one final blink and one giant yawn.

Buzz. Buzz. Buzz.

"What now? Is that my phone? I rushed down the hallway, the sunshine lighting up the living room, a sign I'd slept for longer than I thought. I glanced at my text: Come now. The radio station is on fire.

RADIO STATION FALSE ALARM

I shouted, my arms waving like a windmill. "Seriously, Reed! Who sends a text that says a building is on fire?"

"I called you four times, and you never answered. It was nearly noon. You scared me. So, I'm here working, keeping us on the air when the calls began rolling into the station."

"What do you mean?" I shook my head like a horse swatting at flies; my confusion and inability to follow Reed's conversation hurt my brain. "I threw my hair in a ponytail, came up here in my sweats, and there's no fire. What were you thinking?"

"Yes, there is. It's this community. People are ablaze with hearts that care. I've never seen such."

"Oh, gosh, Reed! Stop talking in riddles. What is so important that you have me up here?" I paused, realizing the coffee pot was clean. "So, you didn't drink coffee this morning?"

"I did, and I cleaned the coffee pot and took out the coffee grounds. But listen, this is important." Reed used his monkey arms to sit me down, pushing my shoulders to the chair at the break room table. "Focus. And stay with me. This is great news. And I must share it with you."

I popped up from the chair. "This week is going too fast for me. And don't ever tell me a building is on fire when it's not. You caused me to lose ten years of my life." I fumed. "So, what's so important that I'm here right this second?" I folded my arms. I wasn't over the panic of the text from Reed that sent my future into flames, even if figuratively.

I had driven like a race car driver to the station, no seatbelt, and with my hair unbrushed, and grabbed a scrunchie from my satchel as I skidded into the parking lot, tossing gravel on the horse, which neighed at me when I got out of Stanley's truck.

Reed sat across from me after encouraging me to sit, and he pushed a paper in front of me. "Take a look."

"What's this? Just tell me."

"It's people calling in pledges." Reed smiled, those yellow teeth lighting the room with his joy. "People are donating to the *Save the Station Fund.*"

"Donations? But we're not having a fundraiser on the air." I turned the sheet around to read it, but I stopped because I was confused. "Hey, aren't you supposed to be running this station?"

"It's fine. Remember Marty? He's from the college radio station and needs some hours. I called him yesterday, and he's agreed to help us out."

"Wait, we can't pay him," I argued, my fingers tapping on the paper under my hand.

"I'm paying him. I have the money. And you know I do. It's my contribution to saving KNBO, even though we won't need it. We do need fresh faces and new blood for the future of this place. Marty's interested in making this his home base. He's that stumpy guy you met at our fish fry. He loves this business."

"Reed, I have to say, you're a great one to stir interest, that's for sure."

"Marty's been here every day this week since he's only working weekends at the college."

I sighed, "So what's with the donations? I don't understand."

"Look, pledges started coming into our call line around eight this morning. Bright and early and with, well, look. See for yourself. Look what I've written down." He tapped the paper like a woodpecker.

I stared, taking in the list. "What? No way. Is this for real?"

"Yes, and Marty's in the booth getting calls, ongoing. Since I came out here to meet you, there's no telling what he's received." Reed inhaled like he'd taken a puff on a cigarette, and his long exhale, one that made me inhale a long relief too.

I put both my hands on the paper. "But how? What started people calling us like this?"

"Well, yesterday, I told our community to keep Stanley in prayer. That he was in the hospital, and you know how news travels. But this is even better."

"What's even better? Will you tell me what is going on?" I wiped my nose, the itch of an answer hiding inside Reed, who took forever to tell stories or anything.

"It's the ladies at the beauty shop. They're pledging money and offering to match other pledges. It's a grand fundraiser by the women."

I scratched my forehead. "But how did they know about our money concerns?"

"Well, early this morning, when I pulled up to the parking lot, Mindy Hinkle—you've met her by now—she asked if we could take some extra phone calls because she was redirecting some hearts at the beauty shop this morning."

"Mindy? Of course, I've met her. She's behind this fundraiser?" I wiped the tear from my eye. "Are you pulling my leg?"

"I'm telling the truth. This is her doing. She wants to do her part in the community. She said she couldn't sing in tune, so being in the church choir is off-limits, but she has a song of hope for KNBO. She said your talk show has encouraged her since they moved here a couple of years ago. She's grateful to you."

I sobbed, "She's grateful for me? How can that make sense? She's got a lot more to be thankful for than my airtime on a talk show."

Reed took my hand from the other side of the table. "When God lets loose a kind soul, the past gets tossed as far as the east is to the west. We have enough to renew our license and keep us going until we revamp our strategy for advertisements and payroll."

"This is hard to take in. I'm at a loss for words."

"So next time I phone you, answer. If we're going to be partners with Stanley and Gladys retiring, we've got to communicate."

"Partners? I never said I'd join ranks with the likes of you." I grinned, challenged by his offer and thrilled at the same time.

"Yes, I know the business. You have the gift of gab. Together with people like Marty and a few others, we can change the landscape of this station and stay on the air. Marty said we need an app for listeners so that they can listen on their phones or computers. So, he's got a friend of a friend, and we're going to see how that unfolds."

"You've been thinking about this before this week, huh?"

"I sure have, Missy. After retiring, I've invested about thirteen years here and have some good years left. I can't hear everything as I should. I can't see those tiny buttons. But I know the business. And I know we can make a go of this if you're with me."

"Yes, I'm in. I want to do this. I can't believe we have money coming in because my new neighbor had an appointment at the beauty shop."

"It's not the beauty shop that was key. Mindy Hinkle is the heart and soul of someone we should all long to be like—she's a fresh voice of hope."

"It's hard to think; she's under so much pressure at home and does this for me." My heart flipped with a life-giving surge, fluttering as if a baby was born somewhere just for moments like this one. I nodded to myself, "Thank you, Jesus, for coming to save us from our sin and ourselves."

Reed agreed, "We have much to be thankful for. Mindy knows what you're doing for her son, Colt, and how that will change his life."

"So, do you know more about Mindy than you're telling me?"

"Sure, I do. Not every thought I have needs to be shared out loud. I'm good at keeping things to myself."

I sighed, "I wish I could learn to control my words."

Reed patted my hand. "You do better than some. Worse than others. Just do the next best thing you can. And by the way, I've taken care of your hospital bill. It seems your insurance wasn't active. I got a call from the billing department after you left the emergency room. They were looking for you."

I rubbed my leg, the pain lessening with each hour. "I know; I hoped that giving them the insurance card would buy me some time." I hugged Reed. "Thank you; I'll pay you back."

"No, you won't. I like you owing me. It's just money. I have plenty, some for your crazy excursions and some for the future of this radio station. Plus, if you owe me, I can get some work out of you." He laughed a squeaky sound through his nose and stood up, towering above me, his thin stature like the tallest tree in the county.

"Reed, you're the best."

He nodded, "I'm not so great at making coffee. It was like syrup this morning."

I smiled at Reed. "Each of us has our strengths. And we each have our weak points."

"Yes, we do. It's time to let our lights shine brighter than the darkness. Together we can make a go of this station for years to come."

"Yes, you're so right. So very right."

**

I parked Stanley's pickup next to my car at the house, holding the steering wheel, sitting amazed at how one day sends me to my knees in fear, while the next props me up and draws me near to God. He reveals His plan through brokenness and songs in the dark. And uses the beauty shop women to change the course of my life.

Off to the side, I watched as Colt hopped from his bike, knocking on the door of a house across the street. He handed a flier to one neighbor, then the next, until he was door-to-door down the block—working as fast as possible.

I jumped from the truck, rounded the house to the side, and ran into Mindy. She leaned on my fence, watching her son. I charged at her, my arms grabbing her neck. "Thank you! I never knew you'd speak such life into so many people so fast. You do change the tide of reckless conversations."

Mindy hugged me back. "It's not much. The best advertisements happen through word of mouth. And a beauty shop is the place to begin such a surge. I hope it helped. I know a few ladies called while I got my hair done this morning, and then I left, going into work late. Sometimes you need a new hairdo. And sometimes a town needs to come together."

I looked at my watch on my arm. "It's three already. I'm going back to the radio station in an hour. Would you like some ice-cold tea?" I peered down the road. "And what is Colt doing?"

"Oh, I made some flyers to tell folks about the fundraiser at the station. He's passing them out on our street. He wanted to help."

Within a few minutes, Colt peddled up to us. "Hi, Ms. Beth. I'm ready to sing my song. I've got all the verses remembered."

I corrected him. "You mean you have them memorized?"

"No, I remember them." He giggled, straddled the bike, and handed the few flyers to Mindy.

Mindy kissed Colt on the cheek. "Thank you for helping us. I will sit on the patio with Beth for a few minutes before your daddy gets back from that job interview."

I opened the side gate, my satchel on my arm, and we moved to the porch. I unlocked my back door, the three bolts in place like I'd left them.

Colt followed us, rolling his bike into the yard. "Can I play in the water sprinkler?" His face, red like a flame, told the story of how hot he was after riding his bike up and down the street.

I glanced at Mindy, and she nodded, so I encouraged Colt. "If you will, that part of the yard needs watering. Let's place the sprinkler beside the storage building to get those dry patches."

He jumped up and down. "And then I can get wet?"

Mindy said, "Sure thing. You're burning up. But wait, you need to take your pump off while you do that, okay?"

I watched Mindy undo the tubing to the injection site on Colt's tummy and then unplug and set the pump on my patio table. "You have fifteen minutes; then this goes back on."

He leaped like a frog, ready to enjoy the water. "Yippee!"

I turned the faucet on. "Give it a second. There's hot water in the hose; let that out first. Then it will cool off."

"Yes, ma'am. I'll wait."

The joy of laughter abounded from Colt, and Beauty hung from a tree branch above him to make sure he didn't get her wet. Mindy and I chatted in the shade of the afternoon heat, the sweat pouring down our backs, the August day, one of the hottest ever, almost like the sun might burst everything into flames.

"This is great. I've not had many people sit with me on the patio."

"I've heard your friend Sally is your closest confidant."

I smiled, "You learn a lot at the beauty shop, huh?"

"Yes, if you listen to a person, you hear more than they say and can pray for everything unsaid."

"Sally's a great friend. She moved back last year, right before her dad passed away. She now runs a home in the country for homeless people and those struggling to find their way. She stays so busy. So, we don't see each other as much as we used to. Plus, she's also managing a business adventure with her daddy's jam. We're getting together next week. Maybe you could join us. We're shopping and going for lunch."

An engine's roar sent Mindy to her feet. "That's Hudson. We must go. Colt, come here. Let's put your pump on. Hurry now. Daddy's back, let's see what news he has for us."

Mindy rushed out the gate, and Colt hopped on his bike. I heard a car door slam on the backside of the fence.

And just like that, the afternoon went up in flames. "Mindy and Colt, where have you been? We're not going to be friends with Beth Bender—she's ruined my life!"

CHAOS IN THE DAYLIGHT

I rushed to the back of my yard, listening in, something I've gotten better at than I knew possible.

Mindy said, "Colt, go inside. Your pump is beeping. Your blood sugar's dropping. Drink half a bottle of apple juice. I'll be right there."

"Yes, ma'am."

For a few minutes, the whispers from Hudson and Mindy were barely audible, and I did my best to grab a word here and one there. Then they spoke louder, and Hudson argued, "How could someone turn me down for a job because he heard I made a harassing phone call to a radio station?"

"But honey, you did make that call. You're letting your temper take over. And words can give life or death in the way we hand them out."

"I'm not going to get a job in this town. Everyone knows I hold Beth responsible for my father's death. And I don't want to, but seeing her sends me to that day!"

"She's a reminder of the loss and the hate you keep close to your heart. But you don't hate her. You hate losing your father. This is consuming you, and Colt is seeing your behavior. He needs good memories, not bad."

"You mean, he needs good memories of me before I die from kidney disease?" Hudson growled, "You know the norm is about five years on dialysis. Five years! What if I never get a transplant? What if I die and leave Colt without a father? I know what that has done to me."

Mindy consoled Hudson. "I know what loss does to a person, too. I'm losing you daily. Your preoccupation with Beth must stop."

"I feel like I'll never recover."

"Then live for Colt. And for me. All we have is what we do today. What will you leave for Colt to hold onto?"

I trampled on my reasons for staying in the backyard, but instead, I ran out the side gate, down the fence to Hudson in the driveway. He cried on his wife's shoulders, a scene that made me skid to a stop.

I eavesdropped, knowing their pain should be private, but I remained. It was as if I were stalking them.

I cleared my throat. "I'm sorry to bother you, but Mindy, you left these flyers on my table on the patio. I thought you should have them."

Hudson wiped his eyes with his hands and stepped to the carport as Mindy came my way. "Thank you, Beth. I think you should go." She lifted her chin to motion that my exit was stage right, left, or both.

I ignored her. "Hey, Mindy, did you tell Hudson about your new job at KNBO? We have twenty hours open for someone to work with me in the evening. Reed, our new station manager and potential owner, wants my talk show to have two women— voices of hope for the evening, for anyone who needs encouragement, and for anyone who needs a friend when life gets heavy. Reed thinks I could use someone to bounce my ideas off, too, and who might bring a fresh take on things."

Mindy frowned but played along, and she glanced at Hudson, who stood, ready to pounce but steady for the moment. "I am twenty-eight. I do have that younger face and the new hairstyle."

Hudson whispered beneath his breath. "You do like to talk."

I smiled. "We'd do great together. Two talkers. Two women who could make a difference and challenge the rest of the ladies in town."

Colt came outside. "Mommy, my sugar is at 45, and I'm dizzy." He collapsed beside Hudson, his feet folding like gummy bears.

Hudson yelled, picking up Colt. "Where's the inhaler?"

Mindy responded, "On the bar. In the gray bag. We can probably get some more juice down him before we need to use it."

They rushed inside, and I stood there—alone, unable to react, unable to do anything except pray. I know we say that we resort to praying when nothing is left for us to do. But we should pray first thing, not last.

I went home, and for what seemed like years, I waited. I waited for my cell phone to ring since Mindy and I had exchanged numbers. I also paced and waited for a conversation at the fence as Beauty climbed higher in the tree. She often senses my tension and stays above me until I calm down. I waited on my porch, but I never saw Mindy again before leaving for work.

I reconciled that since no ambulance came, and they never left, it was good news for Colt and his blood sugar. That also told me the incident ended without severe consequences. Except it took my breath away—in a way that I hadn't felt in years.

Now, it was time to tell Reed I'd offered Mindy a job with me on the talk show. I marched into the station, ready to lay it out for him. "Hi, Reed, I have more great news for you. I've given Mindy a job at the station. She'll work alongside me on my talk show. What do you think about that?"

Since he'd met me at the door, Reed motioned for me to sit down on the lobby's couch.

"What's going on now?"

"We've hit a bump in our journey."

I melted into the soft cushion as if I might sink to the floor. "It's not Stanley, is it?"

"Yes, it's not good either." Reed held my hands like earlier, but this time the gingerly grasp felt more like grief oozing from the way he stared at me.

"What is it? You can't just sit there and not say a word."

"I don't know how to say it. The concussion from the fall caused more damage than the doctor thought, and he's not responding, and there's a brain bleed. He's unconscious but breathing. Gladys called, and they're watching Stanley in the ICU."

"But he only had a few stitches on his forehead. I have more in my leg than he received."

"He's up there in age. I'm not too far behind, and falls can be rough. But right now, we're praying for a miracle. And for healing."

"I need to go see him." I stood, only for Reed to pull me down next to him.

"No, let's keep this station going for him. I need you to pull more weight, and I'm going to hire someone else, along with Marty. I need a full-time employee. What do you think?"

"What do I think? Did you not hear what I said when I came inside? I hired you as the perfect person. I've hired Mindy. But I told her twenty hours. She works at a radio station in Texarkana and has done it all. She can make commercials, record what you need, and knows her way around a radio station. The money she'd save on gas for her car would make it worth her taking a permanent job with us by not driving the twenty-two miles."

Reed pursed his lips. "So, you're going behind my back and thinking for yourself?"

"Yes, it happened without me knowing it would."

Reed hugged me. "Good for you. Great first assignment."

"Wait, you never assigned me a job to hire someone."

"Well, I was about to, but you've exceeded my expectations."

I chuckled. "Reed, they broke the mold when you were born. But I have a question, you've been here for years and never took the initiative to run this station before. What's up with that?"

"This was Stanley's dream. Always has been. I came along for the ride after retirement, and, well, his dream took over my life. Stanley's got a big personality for a short, round guy. But his love for life became my old-age dream, and I want to save this place for him."

"You're a great friend. I want to be like you when I grow up."

"Now that's too big a dream for you. Maybe you should try something more realistic, like calling Mindy and offering her a full-time job. This way, you two can see how it comes off on air—see if the dynamics work and if you complement each other."

"Hey, where did we end up with the pledges today?"

"Let's just say, this community knows how to bless us. We'll be fine for years to come after just this one day. I've gone on air to thank everyone and let them know the fundraiser ends tomorrow at midnight."

I squinted my eyes as if that made me look more intelligent. "So, again, how much did we raise?"

"I've lost count. But a generous donor has offered us $100,000 in addition to today's pledges. This will keep the station going, with one catch. The person who pledged the $100,000 said you must stay on your talk show."

"Now you're making that up. No one pledged that much money. It's a talk show that hardly anyone listens to, except for ladies at the beauty shop."

"Do I look like a guy who would lie to you about such things?"

"No, but who has that sort of money?"

"Well, no one we know." Reed held back the name, but somehow, I knew he wasn't telling me for a reason.

I shook my head, almost in disbelief. "I'm shocked that a little conversation at a beauty shop spread so fast."

"I've always said if I had a secret, I wouldn't tell it in a barbershop or a beauty shop." Reed shuffled down the hall with me right behind him, his giraffe legs long, his steps one to my three.

I pulled on Reed's shirt, worried about Stanley's head injury. "Do you think Stanley's going to pull through this?"

"He's a tough old coot. He'll get better in no time."

"I'm calling Mindy. I should have checked on her earlier, too, because her son had an incident."

"An incident?"

"Yes, he has juvenile diabetes."

"Oh, but doesn't Hudson have diabetes, too?"

"He does, ever since high school. And Colt was diagnosed last year at six. Gosh, I should have called to check on him."

"Well, call her now."

"I am." I dialed her number on my cell. "I need to be a better friend, but I'm used to being by myself. Poor little Colt, his sugar dropped while I was at their house today."

The phone rang in my ear.

Reed asked, "You were over there, and Hudson didn't mind?"

"Well, I was in the driveway, but as for Hudson caring if I came over, he wasn't probably thrilled too much about it." The call connected. "Hey, Mindy. How's Colt?"

"He's fine. Apple juice, then some applesauce, brought it right up. Sometimes it goes low in a hurry."

I swallowed hard. "I didn't know how to help earlier, and I should have called. I was afraid I'd get in the way."

"Well, Hudson might have tossed more anger your way. And we don't need that."

"I was afraid to interfere."

"Well, I'm glad you called. He's much better. Colt's pump beeps to tell him when his blood sugar is low, but he's gotten great at ignoring it."

I listened while she filled me in, enlightened to hear that Hudson consoles and holds Colt when life gets scary.

I added, "I'm so thankful he's okay. I'm not used to dealing with blood sugars. You'll need to educate me."

Mindy assured me that I could learn what to do when Colt's blood sugar drops and how to consider more insulin when it's high. I waited for her to take a breath after the lengthy explanation, my tone almost begging. "Would you mind coming tonight? I go on air at ten, and it's only six. We could wing it and see how the show goes. I'm in the book of Genesis and talking about Joseph. If you want to read up on him, I thought we'd talk about life in the pit and having faith in God during our trials." I poured out my wish for her to join me in one long breath.

"I'd love to come. I'm nervous as a kitten stuck in the tree, though."

"You'll do great. That means you'll take the job and work with me?"

"Yes, it's a great way to break away the stones around Hudson's heart. He'll see how nice you are."

I sighed, thankful she said yes, but worried about how Hudson might react in the long run. "Oh yeah, and it turns out we need a full-time employee if you're interested."

**

At the station, I showed Mindy around. "Welcome to my world. This will be great. I've set up an extra microphone for you. I have some notes too. If the calls come in tonight, we'll chat with friends. Since we've had a little fundraiser today, we'll have more late-night listeners."

Mindy rubbed her hands as if they itched and sat down across from me. "My deodorant isn't working. I'm sweaty in places that don't sweat."

"Don't worry. We'll talk with our callers as if we're in my backyard or your driveway."

"I've not been live on the air before. I've had my voice on recordings, and we get to do retakes. If I mess up, it's out there. I can't believe Hudson agreed to let me do this. That's progress for him. Plus, since he's at home with Colt, this makes it easier."

"We're on in five minutes. Just talk like we're having mango tea on my patio."

Mindy nodded, biting her lip. "I'll let you lead the way, and I'll follow. This is new for me."

"You'll be fine. I've heard you argue at midnight with the best of them."

Mindy laughed, her face flushed. "Life can get loud, especially at my house."

"Here we go. I'll count us down. Three two one." I swallowed and took a deep breath. "Welcome to KNBO with Beth Bender, and yes, we have a new cohost, Mindy Hinkle, joining our show. Everyone, call us and give her a nice welcome."

The first line lit up. The second, then a third. "Mindy, why don't you answer the first line and see who's calling?"

"Hello, this is Mindy with KNBO. What's on your heart tonight?"

The caller's voice filled the station's airwaves. "I'm Kenzie. Last month at the beauty shop, I met you, Mindy, and someone said you married Hudson, whose father died in a car wreck when he was ten. I lost my mother to drugs. I was twelve. I've always wondered what she'd look like if she had lived. I'm twenty-five now, married, and a mom myself. I have three girls. And a great husband. Will you pray that I remain strong for my daughters?"

Mindy whispered into the phone mic. "Can we pray on the air?"

I spoke into my mic. "If you're listening tonight, we will pray for Kenzie and give her some verses to stand on. Mindy, will you lead us in that prayer?"

Mindy sighed, her deep exhale like a teapot steeping flavored tea. "Kenzie, I often feel overwhelmed and inadequate as a mom. I have one son. He's my joy, but I often focus on my weaknesses and mistakes instead of the blessing of his laughter, his way of enjoying life, and the fact that he's a gift to our family. So, yes, I'll pray for you."

I interjected. "We all feel overwhelmed at times."

Mindy prayed, "Lord, please fill Kenzie with your grace so that she may be restored and renewed in her role as a mother.

Help her remember that she's not alone—that you, God, are with her to strengthen and guide her. Amen."

Mindy spent a few minutes chatting with Kenzie after Kenzie mentioned the car wreck. "Yes, I did marry Hudson. When he lost his father that day, well, it was hard. He and his father were fishing buddies, and Hudson stayed home that day instead of fishing. If he'd gone, he would have been in the car—when …" Mindy stopped talking, choking on the rest of her words, her panic evident.

I finished the conversation. "Kenzie, this is Beth. My late husband, Rhett, was the driver who caused the wreck. He left our home after drinking too much, and after he held me against the wall in a chokehold. He packed a bag and wanted to save me from himself. He was afraid one day; he'd go too far." I cleared my cracking voice and continued, "I've never said that on the air before. The day he caused the wreck was the worst day of my life. That was twenty years ago. My future was ahead of me. But my bruises and injuries were more prevalent than his love for me."

Kenzie's voice quivered as she spoke. "I'm thankful for you and Mindy. Most people act like they have it all together, but life hurts, and sometimes it's unbearable."

Mindy and I spoke at the same time. "Amen to that."

I passed Mindy a couple of verses on a sheet of paper, and she read one to Kenzie. "Behold, children are a heritage from the Lord, the fruit of the womb a reward. Psalm 127:3."

After a few more minutes, I wrapped up that call. "Kenzie, we're thankful for you and your girls and, of course, your husband. Our children are a heritage. What a blessing they are to a family. And thank you for calling to talk with us."

"Thank you both. I'll tell others about your show too."

"Thank you so much." I gave Mindy a silent air-high-five of approval.

I sensed purpose in having a cohost and loved how we connected, even with our first caller. Mindy's nervousness faded as she encouraged Kenzie, even though her voice quivered a bit.

I nestled into my chair, tapped the keyboard, and tuned in to the airwaves. "Welcome, listeners. Mindy is picking up line two. Tonight, we'll spend a few minutes taking a road trip with Joseph. If you have your Bible, turn to Genesis 37. I've read this passage, and we see that Joseph was well-loved by his father. So, my question for you tonight is, who had a great father? Or who might be brave enough to share about your father if, well, he didn't live up to his role?"

I read a short passage about Joseph, a teenager with dreams. "Joseph shared his dreams with his brothers, and their jealousy took over, especially because they saw that their father loved Joseph more. Listeners, we don't like to talk about the ugly, only the good. And opening with us on a phone line, especially a radio show, can't be easy. But Mindy and I want to be your friends, so take a walk with us."

While a commercial played, I encouraged Mindy. "You did amazing. It was like we've been doing this together for years. Thank you for doing this with me." I hollered at Reed, who had stepped inside the booth. "Hey, can you get me my notes from my satchel from the break room? I wrote down some new verses."

"Sure thing." He gave me a thumbs-up, popped out, and was right back.

I glanced over at Mindy, who had a caller on hold. "I can't do this. I just can't. I thought I could, but I can't."

I muted my mic. "Why, what's changed?"

"I'm having a panic attack, I guess. I can't catch my breath. This is too real. I'm overthinking now. What if Hudson's listening? He'll get mad and cause a scene."

"Then I'll take this one. I should have taken the lead better. It will work, you'll see. I'd bet Hudson's fast asleep." I pressed the button, taking us back to the live feed. "Welcome, friends. It's Beth and Mindy. We want to encourage you if we can. Let me see who's been holding on line two. Yes, is the caller there?"

"Yes, I'm here. I'm Heather." She paused. "That's not my real name. I don't want anyone to know I'm calling. But I could use someone to talk to."

"So, are we talking about your dad tonight?" I could hear her breathing, and I added, "I'm your friend. No judgment here. Just two friends who are sorting through life and seeing how we can honor God along the way."

"I haven't told anyone. I should have, I suppose. But my dad throws his beer cans against the wall when he's mad. And it could be something like not having butter for his bread or not enough milk that causes his temper to go crazy."

"Let me ask you, Heather, how old are you?"

Mindy whispered away from her mic. "Be careful what you say to her."

Heather responded, "I'm twelve. My little brother is five. Our mom works nights, and I get our supper. Daddy is passed out on the couch, and my brother is asleep. I've listened to your radio show almost every night for months. You help me. Your voice is calming. It's good not to be alone."

Mindy snickered, her hand on her mic. "Calming? Beth Bender is known for that?"

I motioned for Mindy to begin a commercial, pointing to the button. "Folks, we'll be right back after a word from our local sponsor."

I muted the call so that only Heather and I could hear each other. "I've got you on a private line now. What is your real name? Do I know you?"

"You know me. We go to church together. I needed to talk to you tonight. I can't keep watching my mom get hit. It's bad at my house. Tonight, my dad shoved David from his chair at supper. I've never seen David cry like that, and he held his arm until he fell asleep."

"Do you think David needs a doctor?"

"He might. I went to check on him, and he cried when I tried to move his arm."

"Can you give me your address? I'm going to send someone over to check on you both. Do you have a relative you two could stay with?"

"Yes, our Nana lives in town. I'll call her. She'll come for us if I ask, but I'll have to tell her why."

I paused, "She needs to know what's happening. And where's your dad, out cold, right?"

"Yes, he's passed out."

"Let me pray for you. Your name is Holly, right?"

"Whoa, you knew my voice?"

"I did after we spoke for a few minutes. I know where you live, too, I think. It's the old Dyer place off Highway 82, right?"

"Yes, it is."

"So, watch for the ambulance and a police officer. They will make things safer tonight. And do call your grandma."

"I'll call her as soon as we hang up. I didn't know what to do. My dad's not a bad man; he gets so angry."

"Well, for now, we'll check out David's arm, and we'll help you, too."

I hung up the phone, made my calls, prayed for the protection of two children abused by their dad, emotionally and physically, and prayed for a mom caught in the cycle of abuse.

While off the air, Mindy added, "So, you knew the girl?"

"Yes, she's in the older children's choir group at church. I've noticed some bruises on her arms, and I've wondered. Then tonight, it was confirmed."

Mindy smiled. "God used your talk show to help Holly and David tonight."

I sipped some mango tea. "I opened a can of worms by talking about fathers tonight. And I didn't get to take the other calls. But I had to help them. David's only five. Who knows what those two children must see and go through?"

Mindy nodded. "By the way, I took the other calls and recorded them for later."

"See, you know how to run the board. That makes you an asset for sure."

"But I'm still worried that I'll mess up."

"You did amazing."

Mindy wiped her brown hair to one side. "I had some great conversations. One woman shared that her dad was a construction worker with calloused hands. And how, when she was around thirteen, he made sure to have his daughter date with her, like taking a walk, going to the movies, or waking up for church when he was exhausted. She's in college now, and her dad is ill and has lung cancer. She's treasuring their time together."

I wiped a tear from my face. "Mindy, you're meant for this. You're a natural at listening and comforting others."

"I've had plenty of practice with Hudson. With our trials, I've tried to listen and be supportive. But some days are outright hard, and they wear me down. This will give me the lift I need, too, knowing I can help someone."

"I'm thrilled. We made it through our first show. Welcome to KNBO."

Mindy smiled. "I can't believe how fast the time went. I'll go to Texarkana tomorrow and give my notice. I'm ready for my new chapter with you and Reed. And who was the other guy, Marty?"

"Yes, Marty's from the college radio station. It looks like we're on the mend with a new staff member in the making. And the donations will keep us on the air."

"I've got to run. I should get home. I don't want to push the time. It took plenty of behind-the-scenes begging for Hudson to keep his word. He tried to go back on his agreement."

"I was worried he might."

Mindy looked at me with tears. "I try not to be too hard on him. Hudson feels so helpless. The boxes of dialysis supplies will arrive in two weeks. He'll have some port in his stomach and go to the dialysis clinic for his training. And his headaches are horrible, like migraines. He throws up more than any person should, not counting the fact that last year he had a stroke."

I gulped, the knot in my throat throbbing. "I'm so sorry. The more I get to know you, the more I'm reminded that my problems are nothing compared to your family's. I need to count my blessings more and trust God in all things."

"I'm a pincushion, though. One second, I cry when something gets to me. That's when I clean the house from top to bottom. I must be careful, though, because when life gets heavy, I want to take naps to get away from all the sickness."

I embraced Mindy. "I'm so glad you've moved next door. I'm amazed how God takes our past and gives us new surprises and new seasons."

A ringing tone made Mindy jump as if startled. She looked at the screen on her cell and answered the call. "Hello. Colt, what's wrong?" She paused as she listened. "Daddy is on the floor? I'll be right there."

NOT WHAT IT SEEMS

I lingered near the back door at home, knowing something had happened inside Mindy's house, but not sure what transpired. An ambulance never arrived, which I thought might. And Mindy never answered the phone after I called. It was like a déjà vu moment from earlier in the day as I wondered what had happened with Hudson this time instead of Colt.

I gave Mindy time to address her emergency before dialing six times. I glanced up at the sky. "Lord, should I go over? Or should I mind my own business?"

A voice by the gate made me jump. "I don't think this is going to work. Having Mindy on your show isn't good for me. On her first night, you have her talking about the wreck as if she knows what I went through—or what it feels like to grow up without a father. Then you go and blame Rhett. You ran him off. I heard you that day. You shouted at him and told him to leave. You told him never to come back."

I looked Hudson over, shocked that he looked fine.

He marched up to me, continuing his rant. "If Rhett had stayed home, my father would have lived!"

I put my hands on my hips. "So, you felt good enough to listen to the show? But Colt said you were on the floor."

"I rolled out of bed. That's all. Colt heard the thump and got scared. He called Mindy before I knew it. Nothing's wrong, except for this radio show thing."

"Don't you ever sleep?"

Hudson shook his head. "No, sleep doesn't come easily. I'm restless."

I raised my hands to explain. "I come home late every night like this. This is usually my quiet time to wind down. And you're over here invading my world again. Aren't you tired of yelling at me?"

"I don't want to argue. I just want peace."

"Well, you have an odd way of showing it."

Hudson sighed. "I saw the light. I knew you'd be up."

"No, you didn't."

"I did. I was pacing in the backyard and could see the porch light." Hudson paused. "Do you know how many times I've driven up and down this street since we moved back? I've parked in my old driveway and gotten out, reminiscing and crying and wishing. I've longed for a childhood that was better without the ..." Hudson stopped talking, not finishing his sentence.

"You can't go on this long. It must wear you out."

"It's not that easy to get over losing my dad. His accident didn't have to happen. Sometimes, when I've driven here late, I hear you talking or praying to God."

"So, you've eavesdropped on me, too?"

"Yes, it just happened, I guess."

"I do pray. As I said, it's normally my quiet time."

Hudson's hands dropped to his side. "I did listen to the show tonight. I must keep tabs on what you talked about, not that I have any control."

"You don't need to worry about Mindy. She's devoted to you more than you know. But Hudson, this is ridiculous. You used to play in this yard, in the water sprinkler. And eat my cookies. And giggle and shoot me with the water hose. We have great memories together. I was grown, and you were a boy; I would have never told you about Rhett hitting me. I hid my bruises from everyone."

"It's your word against his. Besides, the dead can't defend themselves, can they?"

I growled. "Is Mindy asleep? Please tell me that you'd never hurt her."

"How dare you? How dare you think I'd put a hand on her? She's my wife. My best friend. She's the reason I take a breath and want to live, other than Colt. I love my family."

"Then act as you love them. Seriously, you're a grown man standing in my yard and screaming at me. You act like a ten-year-old!" I backed up, my mouth taking over, my words slipping from my lips like melted butter on burnt toast. I had joined in with Hudson's temperament, losing the battle with my ability to stop raising my voice.

Hudson barked, "I don't think the radio show is good for Mindy. We need the money, so I thought I could let her take this job. But I don't think it's going to be possible."

I argued, "She helped people tonight. She helped them! Do you hear me? She is the best part of you. Don't ruin this for her."

He stormed in a circle. "Then why?"

"Why what?"

"Why didn't you read my email? Every year, you send me a scripture or two. But not this year! You didn't even respond. By not responding, it's like you're saying you've forgotten."

"Forgotten? I lost my husband that day! I lost my future for having his children. How dare you?" I threw up my hands, screaming like a night owl, making enough noise for the owls in the next county to hoot along. "Hudson. You've tossed out threats at me on the radio. And you keep showing up, and it's almost like you're stalking me. I'm not doing this dance routine again. I'll never open the email. Not ever."

"But you must open it. Please, just read it. It's not what you think. This year was different. Or I planned for it to be. You must read it. Or I'm going to explode."

"Going to explode. Are you listening to yourself?" I shook my head. "You are exploding!"

Hudson tracked his steps back to the gate. "Darkness comes. The light will return. I'm falling into the pit of my childhood. And I'm sick. Sick! I'm not going to see my son grow up. Life isn't fair. It's not!"

I inched closer. "I know. It's not fair. But … you're here now. Be the father you've missed. Be there for Colt, no matter what time you have left."

"It's too late. I've let the past ruin my future. I've given them my wounds, and I can't heal. I've tossed them the garbage of my hate. I'll have a good day, only to let them down for weeks on end. I'm weak. I'm frustrated. I'm not the father I should be. I've failed." Hudson put his hands to his face, weeping in the shadows as he swung the gate wide, and he stormed off, leaving me alone in the yard.

I knelt, my body beaten down by life, at a loss for what to do. I glanced at the sky, the darkness a deep black except for the sparkle of a few stars. They winked at me with their light, and I cried like a baby. "Lord, how can I help? What's to become of this situation? Stanley's in the hospital. Hudson's broken from his past and worried about his health. Mindy's the glue for their family, and she had a job with me for one night, and now Hudson has pulled her away. And there's Colt, in need of a father who leads and loves—but ripped apart by the dynamics of this revolving door of pain. What can I do to help? How is this within your plan?"

I offered my gaze to the Lord, but no quick answer came, and no real solution was at hand. I wandered into the house, stepped into my office, and sat at my desk. I used my Touch ID to wake up my computer, moved the mouse, pointed to my email, and clicked to open the app. "Should I read it? I wasn't going to. I don't want to. But I must see what Hudson sent me. He said it was different."

I stared at the screen. Beauty wiggled in and out between my feet, meowing with a sleepy cry. "Girl, in a minute. I've got to read this."

The email popped open on the screen, my eyes scrolling the lines of text, and my heart pounded in my throat. The phrases were like those of a boy who never said goodbye to his father. "Wait, the thumping sound, that's not my heart. It's coming from out back. Surely, Hudson hasn't returned."

I charged down the hallway, storming to the kitchen, peeking through the blinds at the sink. "What is he doing now?" I bent my neck. "What is he doing at my bird feeder?"

I unlocked the door, racing across the yard. "Hudson Hinkle. Go home. What are you doing?" I looked around the yard as if I had trespassed, but I was in my yard. Even though I'm acting strange, and it's about one in the morning. "Hudson, I'm talking to you."

He spun around, holding the bag of birdseed. "You had this bird feeder when I was a boy. You let me fill the container with seed." He gulped, his gasping breath a sign of his possibly crying.

"Hudson, we can't do this. I thought I was clear. You can't keep showing up at my house and in my life. I can't function with this chaos."

"After I went home, I saw the bag of birdseed that Colt asked me to buy. We didn't have the extra money for it, but he wanted to feed your birds. Then I forgot to let him. I'm just keeping my word to him." Hudson put the feeder back on the hanger.

"Go home; I need to go to bed. And stop trespassing." I froze as Hudson crumpled to the ground.

I found myself with my hand on his shoulder. "Hudson, we need to sleep. You need to take care of yourself. You should go home. Please, go home."

Then a shadow joined him, and Mindy consoled her husband. "Honey, you're wrong about Beth. She's not responsible for your loss. You can't keep living with this anger. It's consuming you."

"I'm not angry at her—not in the end. I'm angry at God. I'm flat out angry at God."

Mindy knelt next to Hudson. "Come home. We can't keep this up. We can't do this every night. I can't do this. Not anymore."

Hudson wept like a child, his sobs bellowing and releasing his pain. "I just wanted her to read the email. With us moving next door, I had to let her know everything. Everything! But she didn't read it."

I interrupted. "I was at my desk and about to read it when you knocked on my door. Just tell me what it said."

"I'm not so sure I can say it out loud."

Mindy encouraged Hudson. "Just tell Beth what you wrote."

"I'm not sure I can say it. I've kept the secret for so long."

Mindy held my hand, and I asked, "Secret? Hudson, you're scaring me. What's the secret?"

Hudson grabbed his head. "My migraine is worse, and my blood pressure is going up. I'm not well."

Mindy helped Hudson stand, and he leaned on her. She put her arm around his waist. "Let me get you home. This roller coaster of emotions isn't good for you—or Beth—or me."

Hudson put his hands to his face, rubbing his eyes, his head jerking in erratic movements. "But that day, when I played in the water in this yard, I stood there splashing in the sprinkler. And that's when I heard her."

Mindy put her hand to his lips. "Honey, that was ages ago. We've rehashed this again and again."

Hudson pushed her arm down. "No! Beth argued with Rhett, and she saw me staring at her. Then they went inside."

"Hudson, you were ten. Look, we're arguing right now. Would you want Colt to hear us?"

"No, you know I want to protect Colt."

Mindy took his hand. "Then come to bed."

Hudson bellowed, "But what I've said tonight, and this week, I can't take it back. What's wrong with me?"

Mindy assured him. "Beth is reasonable. She knows you hated losing your father. But honey, I don't want to lose you. We've got to get you help. Your pain is speaking in your behavior. I need you. This is hard for me, too."

"I've talked to the therapists, three of them. I'm not going to another one."

"Come with me. We'll put this behind us soon."

Hudson held the side of his face. "My head is killing me."

Within seconds, Mindy ushered Hudson away, and the gate latched again. I stood alone in the backyard once more, my emotions raw with fear, yet my desire to read the email was in high gear.

I charged into the house, sat at my desk, and soaked up every word. My disbelief at what I read sapped my strength—a boy-man confession in an email, a weight he'd carried for too long—and to think, he had a desire to share his burden with me.

I wiped my nose with the back of my hand, the light of the computer screen glaring in my face. "Hudson, you poor boy. No child should have had to carry such a weight. Now I see that the heaviness of the secret tried to escape, but with every conversation we've had, the past shredded you apart. It's as if you could only launch cannons of pain at me instead.

Thump. Thump. Thump.

I jumped to my feet. "What was that? Is someone in the backyard again? No one is there. No one, surely." I cracked open the door. "What in the world?"

I should have checked the camera footage on my app, but going in person made more sense. I tried to see, my eyes like a beacon searching the yard where a lone star shone a light on the stack of sprinklers. I moved to one. "What is all this?"

Hudson remarked. "It's ... it's your water sprinklers. They're lined up next to each other. I'm searching for the one from ... from that day."

I lost my breath, the air burning my nose. "Hudson, I'm not sure I have the one you played in. That was a long time ago."

Hudson picked up one.

I glanced to the side of the yard. "Did you break into my storage building?"

"No, it was unlocked. I went inside and couldn't see, knocked over a few things, and found the sprinklers."

"I thought you had a migraine."

"I do. But I still can't sleep."

"Hudson, you're pushing the limit. I'm going to have to call the police. You can't keep coming over here. This isn't normal. This is my property."

"I haven't been normal since I was ten. I don't know how to be like the rest of you." Hudson dug through my sprinklers. "I can't find it. I can't find the right sprinkler."

"That's it. I'm calling the police!"

**

I stood on the front porch, keeping my distance from the police car where Hudson sat in the backseat. I muttered under my breath, "I couldn't let the situation continue, and I didn't want to make the call, but I was unable to get him to leave—so Hudson left me no choice but to phone for help."

Mindy nodded, unable to say a word, tears rolling down her face.

I decided to pray for Hudson in a whisper. "Lord, please take the heartbeats of our past and bring peace. Search me. Please help me understand. Add your touch to this mess. I fell apart tonight, as did Hudson. Please, Lord, bring life again. Heal Hudson's heart."

Movement from beside the house made me back up, and I noticed Colt looking under my hedge. He hollered, "Harry, where did you go?"

I leaned around the bushes. "Who's Harry?"

Colt announced. "He's my puppy. Mommy let go of my hand and said, Daddy's better, that he's just resting in the police car. But I can't find Harry."

I mustered a smile, staring at Colt in his flannel Christmas Grinch PJs and his crocs, his attire out of place for August. He folded his arms, his blue eyes bright like the sunrise; the porch light added sparkle to his gaze. I patted his head. "Your dad's having trouble sleeping. He'll be better soon."

Colt asked, "Did you see Harry?"

I glanced around the front yard. "I didn't know you had a dog."

"He's been at the vet, getting medicine. He had to stay there this week because he got sick from something he ate in the trash, and he started throwing up. He swallowed too much grease, I think."

"So, what kind of dog is Harry?"

"He's a long-haired chihuahua. He's black with brown paws." Colt put his hands into a small rectangle. "He weighs three pounds. We got him last Christmas, and he weighed one pound. He came home with medicine from the vet, too, in case his blood sugar dropped. He's like daddy and me. But he doesn't take insulin now. He got better."

"That's great. Let me see if we can find him."

"Here, Harry. Here, boy." Colt looked beneath the hedge and under my car.

We called for Harry, and within minutes, the dog ran toward me. "I think he likes me." I cradled the pup and handed him to Colt.

"He does like you. Mommy says everyone likes you." Colt grinned, a welcome sight for the middle of the night.

The officer came my way. "So, I've got this right. You're not pressing charges?"

"That's right. I'm not. I can't. But I needed to get Hudson's attention."

Colt tilted his head, taking in the conversation. "My daddy's sad. I wish I could go back in time."

I ran my fingers through Colt's blond hair. "Why would you go back in time?"

"Well, I'd find a scientist and help him find a cure for juvenile diabetes. I'd make sure it tasted like cheese pizza, too. Then my dad wouldn't be sick, and he wouldn't need a transplant."

I sighed, "What a great reason to go back in time."

"If I could go back in time, I would also have my grandpa drive home from fishing another way so he wouldn't have a wreck. Then he would be here with us. Then my dad might cry less. I don't like to see my dad cry."

I wiped my tears. "I wish I could go back in time, too."

"What would you change?" Colt begged, his gaze intense.

"I'd change plenty, but we can't do that, can we? We must do the best we can with the path we're on."

"Mommy says courage doesn't mean you're not afraid, but you don't let fear stop you."

"Your mom is pretty smart, I'd say."

The officer pursed his lips and spoke to Colt. "I hope your dad gets better soon."

I nodded as if the officer read my mind, but said it aloud to make sure. "Please, if you will, let Hudson go home with his family. Mindy assured me that he promised to stay off my property."

Colt kissed Harry's head. "Can I still come to see you sometime?"

"We'll work on that part. I'll see you at church Sunday, and don't forget to practice your song."

"I've got it down." Colt petted his pup, who growled a playful sound as though he, too, could sing a verse or two.

Mindy held Hudson's arm as he unfolded from the patrol car, and they disappeared around the house to their driveway with Colt skipping behind his parents.

I sighed. "Thank you, Officers."

One tipped his head like a salute, while the other squinted his eyes, and the two patrol cars drove away. With only a few hours until sunrise, I could get some sleep.

I collapsed on my bed, hugging my pillow, my mind racing, and a twilight sleep set in, half awake and half dozing; my dream state gave way to my standing on a creekbank with a bucket, and Hudson was there too, with a bucket.

We were trying to empty the rushing river from the onslaught of the water; it was like a dream became a symbol of trying to avoid pain, death, and sorrow in life. Above us, the waterfall kept the river full, and our attempt to rid life of trials and tribulations became a wasted attempt. Then a mockingbird landed on a twig by a bush, whistling the tune of every hymn I'd ever heard, all at once, chirping in the wind.

I was startled from the dream, and the four hours of sleep left me wanting more, but the sunrise, bright behind the blinds, called to me. The day of new beginnings was upon me. I found myself humming for the first time in years. I became a mockingbird; my desire to persevere meant letting go of the imaginary bucket of my past. The trials will come. But the strength for my life comes from a God who chose me, and I long to walk in trust.

It's time to move forward with meaningful, intentional steps despite this week's endless reminders of loss. Or the reminders of a past I can't change. We all have secrets. We all have regrets. We all hold the heavy bucket on certain days. I must focus on what I have left. And what I can do to make a difference today.

I picked up my cell phone from my dresser, glancing at the notifications. I had six missed calls from Gladys. And four from Reed.

ALWAYS A PREACHER

I knocked on the door at Stanley's house, not waiting for Gladys to let me in, and I raced inside. "Where is he? He can't be here! He was on his deathbed. I can't believe he's fine, that the brain bleed has stopped. Are you sure nothing's wrong?" I hovered in front of Gladys like a helicopter, my arms rotating in circles, and I spun around. "Where is Stanley?"

Gladys put my arms to my side. "He's fine. He'll have a scar, but he'll be as good as new in a few days. As for you, slow down, Missy. Stanley's got company in the den. He's counseling someone."

"Right now? He just got home from the hospital. He needs the rest so he can get well and come back to work at the radio station." I darted down the hallway toward Stanley's office.

Gladys shuffled with a swish in her worn loafers on the hardwood floor behind me. "Wait, don't interrupt them."

I held the doorknob. "Who's in there? Stanley doesn't counsel people anymore, does he?"

"He does when the call comes in for his help."

Gladys stepped between the door and me. "Come with me. I have coffee in the kitchen."

"Just one hug. I need to see his eyes and see his face." I barged into Stanley's office, skidding to a stop.

Stanley sat behind his desk, shaking his head, his hands wrapped about a giant cup of coffee.

My eyes were glued to Stanley. "You are here. And alive!" I charged to his side, holding him with a bear hug and crying. "Don't ever scare me like that again. I need you with me. I can't function when I don't talk to you every day."

Stanley cleared his throat. "Beth, I'm fine. A bump on my head and your cat tripping me aren't going to stop me from living. Not yet anyway."

I glanced at the person sitting in the chair across from us. "I'm sorry …" I stopped apologizing when I saw Hudson's face. He stared at the floor, not making eye contact. "What? Are you getting counseling from Stanley? My Stanley?" I shook my head, moving to the side of the desk. "It's not even noon, and you're already here bothering Stanley? I don't understand."

Hudson folded his hands, not responding to my interrogation.

Stanley took over. "I've known Hudson since he was a boy. He came by. We started talking. That's all."

Hudson nodded. "Stanley was my pastor, too. Plus, Mindy had me bring him a casserole."

I mouthed, "So Mindy knew Stanley was home before I did?"

"She's connected to those ladies at the beauty shop. One of them called her this morning. They keep up with everyone."

I gave him a slight nod as the near-normal conversation unfolded. "Reed called me earlier, too. But I slept in. Last night was rather chaotic in my neighborhood."

Gladys piped in. "I called you first this morning, too, but you never answered. And I kept calling."

"I know. I was out like a light. Last night, I fought the waterfall of endless problems and didn't get much sleep." I squinted and glared at Hudson.

Hudson licked his lips. "The nights are the hardest. There's no light. I can get lost in the dark."

Stanley stood, turning me toward the hallway. "Let me finish my talk with Hudson, and we'll have some lunch."

I sighed. "Yes, it's been a long couple of days. I'm so glad you're home." I reached around Stanley's neck, kissing his bald spot next to his stitches.

He kissed my cheek. "I'm glad to be home, too. I feel like I've slept through a month of Sundays. The last thing I remember is arguing with Beauty; then the furball got under my feet." Stanley patted his head. "I'm still thankful to be here. I'm getting too old to wallow on a tile floor headfirst."

"You're our rock, Stanley. We rely on you. I'll wait in the kitchen with Gladys. Then we'll eat and catch up."

I left the room, not giving Hudson a goodbye or glance or one more reason to speak—and shut the door behind me. The tears of too many years ran down my face, and my knowing Hudson's secret from his email weighed on me like a boulder.

Gladys motioned for me to join her in the kitchen. "Come with me. I've got the coffee ready, and it seems you and Reed have been up to no good. He's buying the radio station, and I've learned Mindy Hinkle handled a fundraiser for you, too. See how fast the tide of defeat can change? The station will live on. And I'm thrilled."

I grinned. "Mindy was great on the show, too. Did you happen to catch it?"

"I did listen in. She sounded at ease."

"Well, it's already over. Hudson won't let her come back. He's all over the place. Mad one second. Flighty the next. A little scary too. He keeps her under his control."

"Grief does something to you. Especially when it's tucked deep inside for years."

"He's holding onto an anchor that keeps him in one place, and it's worse than his simply losing a father. He keeps telling me he blames me, but his email said something altogether different. I think he blames himself."

Gladys poured me a cup of the darkest coffee, a Cajun brew she loves. "Here, drink this. The cream's in the fridge. I've got to switch out the laundry. I'll be right back. Then you can tell me more."

She slipped to the adjacent room, humming, and I found myself eavesdropping outside Stanley's office while grasping my mug.

Stanley asked Hudson, "I didn't think you were close to your dad, and from what you've told me, he was hard on you and your mother."

Stanley's words sounded harsh, even to me, but he has a way of getting to the core of problems.

He went on. "The loss of a parent is a loss of memories. But for you, as a victim of your father's abuse, it's the loss of hope, too. You and your mother lost the future of what you hoped might happen when your father died in the wreck. With Rhett and Peter being brothers, it complicated your relationship with Beth, too."

Hudson whispered, "I've caused so much turmoil, not that it was the right thing to do."

Stanley added, "Peter and Rhett grew up with abuse and endured some rough days. Their father lashed out with his hands and his words, and they learned to treat others the same way."

I swallowed as if a lump of charcoal burned my throat. After Rhett died, I returned to my maiden name. Being a Hinkle didn't fit anymore—and in time, everyone got used to calling me Beth Bender. Even my mailman preferred my maiden name.

Hudson broke the silence, and I leaned on the door, listening. "I always had the desire to make some happy memories with my dad. We had a few good times when he didn't yell or hit my mom. And we did fish together sometimes. I miss what I never had: a normal day without fear and anger. And now, look at me. I'm the angry one."

Stanley countered. "When you were small, you escaped by going to Beth's backyard and playing. You were free there."

"I know, until that day, I loved being with Aunt Beth. She played with me. She baked for me. She was good to me. But then I heard her and Uncle Rhett arguing that day. It was like I was hearing my dad scream at my mom."

I put my back to the wall, soaking up the private conversation of a man trapped as a ten-year-old. He shared most of what he had in my email.

Hudson remarked. "I didn't go to my dad's funeral. I argued with my mom until she gave in. I didn't want to be there, where people were going to pretend that my dad was a good person. No one had any idea of what he did inside our home."

Stanley asked, "If you had gone to the funeral, would you have felt like he was controlling you?"

"Yes, he would have the final whisper of hate in my ear. I had all these thoughts about how I felt —loving him one second, mad at him the next. But even now, I would give anything to have him back."

"Your dream to have your father would be him as a peaceful and kind man, without the screaming and the fists, right?"

"Yes, I would love to go back in time."

"But you've told me that you're mad at God, too. Why is that?"

"Because God let this happen. He could have stopped the accident. He could have saved my mother from the horror. But he didn't."

"So, are you going to blame God for how you're treating Colt and Mindy?"

"Wait, I don't hit them. Never have."

"But your rage is growing. Something must change."

"You're right. I know that. That's why I'm here. I need to make changes to show them how much I love them."

Stanley went quiet. Hudson too.

Then Hudson said, "But by not going to the funeral, I didn't pay my respects."

"I'm pretty sure there's no record of Jesus ever attending a funeral. He attended weddings and feasts, and he raised people from the dead, but I don't know of his going to a funeral. So, let's pray for the Lord to raise you from the past, that you might live."

"Have I become my father?"

"No, not if you live in the light and love of Christ. With Jesus, you have hope."

"But I'm saying one thing and then doing another. And now the diabetes is winning, and I'm starting dialysis soon. My kidneys are functioning at ten percent. I don't want to leave this world and inflict emotional scars on Colt. I want to leave him with good memories."

"Well, you're not dead yet. Your greatest dilemma is the internal one that no one sees. You struggle with letting go of the longing for a father's love. And God is there to remind you that He is your Father—always."

"I wanted my dad to love me, to value me. To support me. To encourage me. To love my mom. To be good to her."

119

Hudson's gut-wrenching sobs made me sniffle with tears of my own.

Stanley added, "When your dad died, you lost the opportunity to see if life might improve for you and your mother. You don't have a beautiful ending to your relationship with your father. But still, you love him. And yet, you have hated him. You have conflicting feelings. You've dug through your past as if panning for gold. You've sifted through your memories; it's time to keep the bits that are worth saving and then release the soot and filth back into the creek bed."

I sat there, taking in the wisdom of Stanley's words as they filled the void of my heart with relief and with hope. I, too, experienced the same abuse as Hudson. But he was a mere boy of ten. At the same time, I was a young woman. And yet, a car accident took two brothers on the same day, leaving family members stranded without answers and hurting for years.

Gladys knelt in front of me. "If I get down here, you'll have to help me up."

"Yes, ma'am." I held her hands, and she crossed her chubby legs, her wrinkles smiling at me as she looked into my eyes. "Gladys, as you know, Hudson sent me my annual email. This year, it was different. It was a confession. After his dad argued with his mom that morning, he blamed himself for letting Peter go fishing. What no one knows is that before Peter left, he threw Hudson against the wall when he tried to stop his parents from fighting—only to get tossed over a chair."

Gladys put her hand to her mouth. "That poor boy."

"That's why Hudson came to my house and played in the sprinkler, not taking off his shirt—he didn't want me to see his bruises."

Gladys wept. "Life can be cruel. But Jesus heals the brokenhearted. And calls you, His child."

I wiped a tear from my chin. "Hudson yelled at his dad that morning and told him he hoped that he drowned in the lake while fishing—and then his father died that afternoon. Hudson lives with those words. And they're consuming him. He doesn't hate me. He hates their last conversation."

Gladys hugged me. "All children deserve love and safety, and they deserve parents who take care of them. But not every father or mother gets it right. It can break your heart."

"Yes, you're so right. So right."

The door next to us flew open, and Stanley appeared, his short stature leaving him closer to the floor than to the ceiling. "Gladys, call an ambulance. And call Mindy. Hudson's struggling to breathe, and he's grabbing his head and mumbling. Something's not right. Not right at all."

BROKEN FORT

The paramedics tried to engage Hudson, but his loss of understanding led to combative behavior. "Sir, let me get your vitals. I'm here to help."

"Where am I? I'm not at home. Where's Mindy?"

A few minutes later, Mindy charged inside and came to Hudson's side. "Honey, take a deep breath. We're going to take you to the hospital."

Hudson folded his hands into awkward shapes, with fingers going one way, his bent arms another. He muttered inaudible words, gasped, and stared at the wall. It's as if the earth stopped rotating, except for the earthquake inside me. It was like everything spun out of control.

I put my hand to my chest, my heartbeat like forty drums pounding beneath my shirt. Beside me, a whimper made me look down, and there stood Colt in a red T-shirt and blue shorts. "What's wrong with my daddy?"

I took Colt's hand, walking with him to the kitchen. "Have you had lunch?"

"I'm not hungry." Colt tore around me, running to the stretcher where Hudson wiggled, arguing with the paramedics. Hudson spewed fragmented sentences at everyone about how

122

he needed sleep and had lost his keys. "Daddy, what's wrong? Please, come home with us." Colt pulled on his dad's hand. "Take me with you."

A paramedic with a long face said, "Sir, try to relax."

The scene slowed like hitting Pause on a remote, and Hudson was inside the stretcher within less than five minutes. Colt cried, then whimpered at the window.

Mindy ran back into the house, touching Colt's chin and kissing his forehead. "I'm following the ambulance. I need you to stay here."

Gladys said, "We'll be glad to keep Colt."

Mindy wiped her nose. "I hate to ask; we don't have family here, and I'm sure the hospital's not going to let Colt come inside the emergency room."

Gladys exhaled. "Sure, we have room for the company any day of the week."

Mindy explained. "He has juvenile diabetes and wears a pump. He knows to listen for the beep to see if his sugar is low or high. I have the app on my phone to monitor his Dexcom on his arm. I'll keep watch and text you if he needs insulin or juice." She started to dash off, kissed Colt on the head again, and hugged him like a momma bear with her cub.

I tugged on Mindy's sleeve, offering my help. "Mindy, I know we've just met, but we are family. Please, let Colt stay with me. We'll get Harry, too. No dog likes to stay home alone."

Colt pressed his nose on the windowpane, staring at the ambulance as it pulled away. "They're taking Daddy away."

Gladys hugged Colt. "He's in good hands. They'll find out what's wrong and get your dad home."

Colt sniffled and put both hands on the glass window. "Daddy, don't go. Please."

Mindy sighed and moved near me. "Are you sure that you don't mind? I appreciate this. I'll keep you posted on what I learn, too." Mindy raced out the door, jumping into her SUV, which was parked in the driveway next to Hudson's car, the one I never saw when I came over earlier.

I inched over to Colt. "Your dad will be better once they run some tests and give him some medicine. And he would want you to eat some lunch." I nearly choked, wondering how to determine how much insulin Colt would need at a meal.

Colt bit his bottom lip, then smacked. "Can we get chicken nuggets and fries and a diet Dr Pepper at McDonald's?"

"Um, yes, we can. But what do I do about your insulin? I've never done this before."

"If we go to McDonald's and get a medium combo with ten nuggets, it's 77 carbs. I key that into my pump. It's easy. I'll show you." Colt lifted his shirt, revealing his pump tucked inside a small pouch on a band at his waist.

"Well then, Gladys and Stanley, I know you have a casserole, but would you like nuggets or a burger today?"

Stanley tapped his belly. "I need to cut back. The casserole will do."

Gladys winked. "He'll eat three helpings, I'm sure. That won't be cutting back."

"I'm a growing boy."

"You're not growing the right way. You're wider than ever."

Stanley laughed. "You're a little rounder too these days."

The two seniors scooted to the kitchen, and Gladys called to me. "If you need anything, let me know."

"Yes, ma'am. I'll take Colt with me to the station. He'll be my co-worker tonight if he can stay awake." I moved toward Colt, who hovered by the front door. I called Stanley back, "I'm so glad you're home. Get yourself completely well, and then I expect to see you back to work."

"I'll be there tomorrow."

Gladys countered, "No, he won't. I'll make sure he rests for a few days."

**

After lunch, I tossed the empty McDonald's bag away, and Colt reminded me, "We need to get Harry."

"That's so right. Come on."

In the driveway, Colt ran to the side door under the carport, punched the code on the security lock, went inside, and came charging out with Harry on his heels.

I waited beside the street by the fence to make sure Colt was safe, and Harry was like a rabbit set loose and ran down the road. "Harry, come here. We're going to my house. Come on, boy."

Harry darted in circles and followed us into the backyard. I knew Beauty might not show herself until Colt and his pup went home—she's not great with dogs. "Did you get your iPad? Your mom sent me a text that you have games on there that you like to play."

"Yes, it's right here."

"Good, but if I have my way, we'll unlock the imaginary key that's by my bird feeder, and we'll set ourselves free for a great adventure." I rustled Colt's hair as he pounced beside me, the sad eyes of a small boy, overcome by his dad's ambulance ride, in need of a distraction.

"Free? I didn't know we were trapped."

"Sometimes you don't know you're in a cage because it's invisible, and you need to open your eyes to see what you're missing."

Colt jumped around me as the gate closed—the cage locking us inside. I tugged on his sleeve. "Watch out. Jump over that spot in the grass; it's a brown place where the grass died from the weeds. If we step on it, we'll sink into the center of the earth, and we'll never have ice cream again."

"I don't eat regular ice cream. But they make it sugar-free with low carbs."

"That's why we need to jump. Come on. Jump now. Hurry. Watch out. Those dead pieces of grass will latch onto your shoelaces and pull you under and snatch your shoes off, then eat your toenails." I jumped two feet ahead, waving for Colt to do the same.

"Ms. Beth, it's only grass."

"No, the toenail monster is pretending to be dead grass. He likes to chomp on toenails for protein. And he'll take the rest of the toenail to the family of monsters hiding under my house in the ground. He has purple eyes the size of oranges, too. Hurry, he'll get you. Jump. Do it now."

Colt giggled, his feet leaping over the patch of dead grass. "I did it. I'm alive. I'm not in the center of the earth. And I still have my toenails."

"If you ever look the monster in the face, he'll pull you under by grabbing you by the ankle—then he'll shoot snail-goo into your eyes. And then go for your feet."

"I don't want to lose my toenails." Colt pursed his lips while Harry chased Beauty in the back of the yard—she darted beneath the storage building to get away.

I clapped my hands. "I'm glad you made it over here in one piece. You're already noticing things you never paid attention to before." I pointed to another patch of grass. "There's another trap. Jump again."

Colt bounced like a kangaroo, with Harry coming our way, circling Colt's every step, a ball of lightning let loose in a three-pound dog. He reached for his dog. "Harry's going to be swallowed up."

"No, not to worry. The toenail monster doesn't like little dogs. Just little boys and old women."

"You're not old like Ms. Gladys. That's old. Her skin on her face is under her chin."

I chuckled. "Well, I do have some of the same skin she does; sagginess comes with age."

Colt stopped talking and held out his arm, pointing with one finger. "Look, it's an orange and black butterfly."

"It's a Monarch. Isn't it pretty? I love how butterflies remind me of freedom."

Colt jumped. "There it goes. Over the fence to my driveway."

I turned Colt toward the oak. "Look, there's a ladder. We can climb the tree and see if there are any other butterflies."

"What if there's only one?"

"Well, let's climb the tree, and we'll see."

Colt bent his head, staring straight up the trunk of the tree. "Is that a fort?"

"It used to be a rocket ship for ... for your dad."

"Really? It looks like a fort." Colt scaled the tree as if a miracle lived inside the walls of plywood and spider webs.

"Be careful. I'm right behind you."

Colt looked down. "Aren't you too old to climb trees?"

"I'm not too old to keep up with a seven-year-old." I hung onto a branch, tailing Colt. He pushed the small, tender branch away from the opening, which looked like a crashed rocket with wobbly boards and warped walls. "Wait, let me make sure it's sturdy. That's been there for years; the wood's weathered and rotten."

He glanced at me. "I'm going to see what's inside."

"No, wait for a second. Let me see first." I peeked into the fort; the brown leaves were packed in a corner, where a dark red string poked from beneath the pile.

Colt stuck his head around me. "What's this?"

I reached for the string and pulled an old baseball from the littered floor of the fort. "Well, look what I found."

Colt sat on a branch. "Is that your ball?"

"No, it's an old baseball. The thread's gone on part of it, and the leather's brown. It must have been your dad's ball. He played up here and used to hide inside, ignoring his mom's calls to come home."

"Can I have it?"

"Sure, it's not much of a ball anymore, though."

Colt held the ball, his fingers clutching a branch. "Is my daddy going to leave in a rocket and go to heaven?"

I wobbled, my foot slipped, and I grabbed the branch. "Your dad's going to pull through this; his body is broken in some ways. But he has great doctors, I'm sure."

Colt got lost in staring at the fort and pointed. "There's the butterfly. It's way up there."

"Yes, I could watch a butterfly all day. But, come on, let's go inside. All this tree climbing is making me thirsty."

"Five more minutes. Maybe my dad will build me a fort someday."

"Maybe he will." I smiled, "Hey, since you'll go to work with me at the station tonight, I'm going to give you a set of headphones. Would you like to become a radio talk show host? We'll call your show: Colt's Show for Kids."

"Do I have to talk?"

"Yes, it's radio. You could talk to some kids."

We mustered the downward slope of the tree's split trunk, jumping to the ground like kangaroos who thought they could climb trees.

"I don't think I want to, but can I go see my dad? I want to see my mom too." Colt clutched the ball, glancing around the yard. "Where's Harry? I don't see him."

"He's here somewhere. Come here, boy. Harry, come on, boy."

A three-pound rocket-dog crawled out from beneath the storage building, dusty from his adventure, content from a nap.

Colt picked up Harry. "Can you take me to my mom now?"

"Oh, honey. I would, but she's at the hospital with your dad. She'll be calling soon to check in. Let's get something to drink."

Inside the house, Harry darted to the couch, to the recliner, and down the hall, and Colt sat on the floor with his back against the sofa, his legs crossed, staring at the old baseball.

I rustled his hair. "Your tea is on the bar in the kitchen. It's unsweet. Aren't you thirsty?"

"No, I just want to go home."

Harry circled me, chasing himself to catch his tail.

Ring. Ring. Ring.

"Hey, that's my cell. I bet it's your mom." I pulled my phone from my jeans pocket. "Hello. Yes. Oh my. Goodness. Seriously?"

My heart raced, my worry growing with each pause as Mindy explained the lesions from the brain scan and how, in the last year—with Hudson's trouble keeping his blood pressure under control—he's had another stroke.

I muttered, "He'll stay a few days in the hospital?" I paused as Mindy asked to speak to her son. "Sure, Colt's right here. I'll give him my phone."

Colt's eyes grew big. "Hi, Mommy."

I plopped down on the cushion of the couch, listening to a small boy breathe and whimper as he soaked up his mother's voice.

Colt cried, "No, I don't want to stay here. Come get me."

He listened to Mindy, and I watched. He begged. And I held my breath. I wanted to console Colt, but the invisible cage of sickness surrounded the Hinkle family.

Mindy must have assured Colt, but I worried about knowing what to do with Colt's blood sugars and what to prepare for his meals.

I slipped from the room with Harry on my heels and opened the closet in my office, where the old shoebox held things for small boys—things from one boy—Colt's dad. I'd saved them all these years, hoping I'd give them to Hudson one day—but life spiraled out of control, and I never had the chance.

The dusty box might hold a little hope for Colt—like a part of his father might jump from inside when the lid came off.

I rushed to the living room, carried the shoebox, and Colt wept, sitting on his knees. He handed me the phone. "Mommy wants to talk to you."

After a few minutes, and with instructions from Beth about what Colt would wear to church this weekend, I promised Mindy that I'd text her with my questions and that I'd keep Colt safe and do my best to make him smile. "Bye, we're praying Hudson's recovery is fast and that he'll be home soon. If you need me, call."

Mindy agreed and said, "There were no physical signs of the stroke, leaving any damage. But since Hudson's here already, they're going to put the catheter in his stomach to prepare for the peritoneal dialysis. So that's good, I guess."

"Yes, one less surgery to have later. We'll be fine. Take care of yourself."

I hung up the phone and sat on the floor in front of Colt, who rocked on his heels, crying. "Sit with me."

Colt obeyed like a robot caught in auto mode.

"Look, I have a treasure chest for you. Well, it's better than a treasure chest. It's a hope chest." I kept my hand on the shoebox. "But first, we must blow away the cobwebs and clear out the dust."

Colt sniffled. "It's just a shoebox."

"But not just any old shoebox." I tapped the box, dust flying. "So, blow with all you have. Let's get rid of the dust from this box, and you'll see—you'll see the treasures inside.

Colt puckered his lips, blowing at the box while Harry sniffed and danced with an interest of his own.

"That's it. Blow hard. Blow with all you've got. The dust needs to go. The hope needs to land. The future is at hand."

Colt touched the lid. "Can we open it now?"

"Yes, but go slow as you touch each item. If you miss what you see, you'll miss what you need because these treasures belonged to your dad."

Colt shook his head. "My dad? Really?" He lifted the lid and placed it on the hardwood floor. "What's this?" He touched an egg-shaped, faded pink item.

"That's a Silly Putty. When I was a girl, we took the putty from inside and pressed it on a comic in the Sunday newspaper, and it copied the print to the putty."

Colt squinted. "Huh? What's a newspaper comic?"

"Oh, it was like a comic book cartoon strip in the paper. And it was in color. Open the egg up. That putty is surely dried up by now."

Colt squeezed, twisted the egg, and a blob of solid putty plopped to the floor like a rock. Harry chased it with his nose; the putty must have seemed like a ball to him.

I reached for an item. "Here, look at this. This is a View Master." I held up the green and blue toy like small binoculars. "You put these disks in here. Each one has a story on it. You push the lever, and it advances the pictures. You put your face on this spot and look inside."

Colt grabbed a disk. "Toy Story and Buzz Lightyear!" It was great to see Colt smile — his joy contagious — and it made my heart sing.

"Look, Ms. Beth. Here's a Buzz Lightyear in the bag from McDonald's. Was this my dad's toy?"

"Yes, he used to leave toys at my house. And he loved McDonald's as you do. He left his things in my yard, on my floor, and by the tree where he climbed high, singing to infinity and beyond."

"Daddy likes to sing?"

"Yes, he used to sing all the time." I heard my words, knowing they were for me too—and somehow, a song slipped from the dusty box of my past, and I let out a squeal. "Hallelujah. Hallelujah."

Colt jumped. "Whoa! What was that?" He chuckled, "You can sing high."

"I guess I can." Harry froze in place as if he'd heard a howl of pain escaping. He growled, and I petted his head. "It's okay, boy. I'm finding my song again."

Colt pointed. "Look, it's a tiny Rubik's Cube. I have one of these."

I picked up a miniature barrel-shaped container. "Guess what's in here?"

"I don't know."

I cracked open the container. "It's a barrel of monkeys." I hooked the long-armed monkeys together. "Look, they're hanging onto each other."

Colt took one red monkey, then another, and held the six monkeys in the air, laughing like a small boy should—even though life tossed a barrel of hard days at him.

I counted the monkeys, giving them names, one for Hudson, one for Mindy, one for Colt, one for Beauty, and one for Harry. And one for me.

Colt nudged me. "Look, Ms. Beth. Three marbles. One is blue, the other green—"

I finished his sentence. "And the other is orange in the center. Those are called cat eyes because of the veins of color."

"I like these. The green is for dad. Blue for mom—she's sad. And I'm the orange one." He clacked them together in his hands. "Cat eyes. Can I keep these?"

"Sure, the whole box is yours. You can show your dad his treasures when he gets home from the hospital."

I got up and went to the back door, looking for Beauty. "Here, kitty. Mommy must go to work. You'll want to come inside. It's too hot for you to stay out there."

Meow. Meow.

Beauty crawled from beneath the storage building, but Harry darted from behind me, and before I knew it, he ran Beauty up the tree to the old fort.

I scolded Harry. "Bad dog. Leave the cat alone."

Colt showed up, holding his marbles. "Harry chases everything. He likes to chase squirrels, too."

"Well, they need to become friends if they're going to be neighbors. Now Beauty's in the tree. I'll climb up and get her."

Colt handed me his marbles. "Hold these. I can get her. I can climb better than Buzz Lightyear."

"Are you sure?" I clutched the marbles.

"I'm good at climbing trees."

In the middle part of Colt's climb, the beeping sound on his pump sounded off.

I hollered, "Does that mean your blood sugar is low?"

"It might. If it gets too low, I'll need to have a cookie or juice or 15 carbs to get it back up."

I called up the tree's trunk. "What happens when it gets too low?"

"I could pass out." Colt's matter-of-fact response didn't help my anxious heart. "There's Beauty, I see her. She's in the rocket."

Beep. Beep.

"You'd better come down. We can't have you passing out—not with me—not at all."

Then a Monarch butterfly of yellow and black flittered between the branches right above me, right before Colt hollered, "Ms. Beth, help me."

COLT'S TALK SHOW DEBUT

Reed met me at the door. "Well, look what we have here. Is this a new employee?"

Colt backed behind me, his shyness kicking in at meeting a man who towered like a tree.

"Tell Mr. Reed hello. He's our owner and manager. Or soon to be."

"Hi, I have marbles." Colt held out his hand.

Reed marveled at the sight. "Look at those cat eyes. I have some like that myself."

I chuckled, "I thought you lost your marbles long ago."

"Funny, very funny."

"Colt and I wiggled past Reed, who looked out the door at the sky. "Today's been cooler. But there's a storm brewing somewhere."

"There's usually some storm brewing on any given day. It's what we do to prepare and how we react when it comes that matters."

"I was talking about rain; you overthink most of what I say." Reed cackled, his teeth causing Colt to do a double-take.

Colt pointed. "My mom says we should brush our teeth, so we don't have cavities."

Reed took notice. "My stains are from too many cigarettes and too much tobacco. I made some choices that left their mark. I've always planned to buy myself some teeth like Stanley did, but never got around to it."

Colt rolled a marble against the wall.

Reed moved closer. "What's with the scratch on your arm? It's fresh. Did Ms. Beth put some medicine on it?"

Colt rolled another marble, clacking it on the green one. "Yes, she did. A branch scratched me when I fell out of her tree."

I interjected. "He slipped from a branch."

Colt gathered his marbles and put them in his jeans pocket. "I passed out."

"You didn't quite pass out." I sighed, grateful for a scratch when it could have ended with a broken arm or worse.

"My blood sugar went low, and I got dizzy."

Reed asked, "And you were in a tree when this happened?"

"Yes, I was after Beauty."

"Beauty? Ms. Beth's cat?"

"Yes, sir. My dog chased her up the tree."

"And Ms. Beth sent you up the tree for the cat?"

"No, she was going to climb up, but I saw how she took forever to get up to the fort the first time—she's too old to climb a tree."

I clapped my hands. "Wait, I'm not too old for anything."

Reed roared, "Beth, you're halfway through your life. Climbing trees is not a great idea. But why didn't you just let Beauty stay in the tree? She is a cat after all."

"I didn't want her to get too hot."

"Didn't you notice that it's fifteen degrees cooler today than it's been this month?"

"No, we were busy chasing butterflies, and cats and dogs, and searching for treasures today, that is, until Colt bounced out of the tree."

Reed nodded. "So, you let the boy fall?"

"I did not let him fall. He slipped down the branches, and I caught him."

"You caught him?"

"I did, I'm good at catching."

Reed laughed, "But you're not good at climbing?"

Colt added, "She's not good at climbing."

I realized Colt and Reed ganged up on me, a sign for me to stop arguing with them.

Reed asked for Colt's marbles. "Let's play a game. I have a few more minutes before I need to get back in the booth. Marty's in there, holding down the fort."

Colt asked, "Who's Marty?"

"He's one of the family—another radio friend."

**

My mind wandered to a land where men are kind like Reed, where men are leaders like Stanley, to a place where voices don't get loud or harsh, where words are inviting. I knew the only place where such things happen was in heaven—where Jesus is kind, where He's a loving leader, where His words invite us to come, where no one gets sick. Or hits. Or cries. Or dies. Or gets chased. Or falls from a tree. Or scratches their arm.

Since I grew up in foster care, I had hoped life would be filled with new songs and kindness. But the journey was challenging, and often loud—not that I helped make it better, I rebelled and hit and scratched at everything people did for me.

There was a time when it all went wrong for me, my dreams shattered by a foster dad who kept his rage from the world. But

137

at home, he fought his way like a Rubik's Cube, unable to match his desires with his actions. He failed to lead or speak kindness into my teenage ears; this was at my fourth foster home.

That's when I ran away, and a school friend's father took me in, in my senior year, so that I could graduate high school. No one came for me. I'll always be thankful to Sally and her father, Max, since I was never missed by the man and his wife from across town. Which made me sad, and still very glad.

I dreamed of love, a family, and children of my own. In Max, I saw a father's love for his daughter, even though Sally's mother died when she was a baby. Their home was a place I longed for—to have of my very own. I'd met a father who was a leader, who spoke with kind words and with corrections. Max expected more of me than I knew I could muster—a year I'll treasure forever.

I often dreamed God would be forgiving during the time I ran off. I was young and afraid—and much like a cat in a rocket fort. I hid from life by running away. Then I found myself in a marriage that brought bruises and scratches, and I felt like no one would catch me if I fell. The scratches were deep like sinkholes where you could fall to the center of the earth—until I met Stanley and Gladys at church.

Now I've spent years daring to dream again, while at times finding myself trapped in the tree with those dreaded emails from Hudson. Now I'm ready not to let another summer slip by. I want the autumn season to change me—because I still have a dream. I still have hope that when storms come, the weather won't kill my future—that my days of singing aren't over. When I sing, it reunites my head and heart with God's heart.

Colt tugged on my arm. "Reed said I get to be a star."

I came back to myself. "A star?"

"Yeah, he's going to pay me too."

"Pay you? For what?"

"For doing the kid thing, you said. You never told me I could get money."

"I thought we'd talk more if it went well." I found myself stuttering and tried not to react to Reed, who stood behind Colt, smiling, his eyes sparkling as if he were proud of himself. "So why does this make you a star?"

"Reed said stars come in all sizes, like we see in the sky."

I remarked, "Reed's like the Big Dipper then, and I guess you can be the Little Dipper." I played along, knowing full well Reed would end up winning—so I gave in. "So, what are you going to talk about on your show?"

Colt held up his marbles. "I'm going to tell people about marbles."

Reed winked. "Great, we have a topic. So, let's have him go on the air with me at five since his age group isn't awake when you're on."

"That's a great idea. I'll send out a notification on my phone to everyone on our station's Facebook page that we have a new talk show host who is seven and is a rising star."

Reed motioned for his buddy to join him. "Come with me. We've got a new show to put on. You'll sit across from me, both of us wearing our headsets. We'll talk about marbles and see if we can give people a few minutes of fun, and maybe, someone might call in and ask you a question."

Colt glanced at me. "What if I don't know the answer?"

"Then Reed will help you. He's going to be with you every step of the way." The station's airwaves went through the building after I adjusted the knob on the wall.

Colt stopped walking. "What if I don't do so well?"

I patted him on the shoulder. "Just pretend you're talking to Harry."

Reed asked, "Who's Harry?"

Colt smiled. "He's my dog."

Reed put his hand on Colt's shoulder. "Let's go talk to the world."

I grinned, patting my pocket, which held Colt's Wi-Fi phone to monitor his blood sugar. "I'll keep track of my star right here."

I moved to the recording booth, ready to tape a few commercials, and sat down, resting in the moment, tired from the week's roller coaster and yet marveling at the ride of connecting with a small boy who reminded me of his dad. The hair. The eyes. The chin. The grin. Colt was the exact image of his father. Adorable. Precious. A gift.

I sighed. That moment reminded me how much I had longed for a child of my own, even now. But I do have children at church who are stars in all shapes and sizes. And they are precious to my heart.

A tap on the door interrupted my daydreaming. Marty stuck his head inside. "Hey, I took the liberty of recording the commercials. I heard your week's been full. I just thought I'd let you know."

I swallowed. "You've already done them?"

"Yes, Reed mentioned you might appreciate some help."

"He did, did he?" I recognized my curtness, and put my hand to my mouth, my stitches in my leg itching. My wound reminded me of how I shouted at a guard, at a neighbor, and how the ups and downs wear a person down—and now, I'm raising my voice to a new coworker.

"Did I cross the line?" Marty ran his fingers through his thick hair, his face twitching as if he'd encountered a bear instead of me.

"No, it's been a rough week. Thank you so much." I stared into the green eyes in front of me, not remembering how

140

Marty's jawline was square, how his face spoke of strength and confidence.

"I'm here to help with whatever you need. Just ask. I love radio and these days, going live and having access to working at this station—it's where I'm home."

I took in his words. "So is radio in your background?"

"Yes, my father was a DJ from way back. And his father, too. It's in our blood."

The speakers caught my attention as Reed's introduction made me pause. I shushed Marty. "Wait, Colt's going to do a little radio with Reed."

"I met the boy. He favors you."

"He shouldn't. He's not my son. Remember Mindy, who worked one night? Well, Colt's her son. And her husband, Hudson, is in the hospital. I'm babysitting."

Marty's bushy, yet perfectly shaped eyebrows raised as he nodded. "Isn't that the man who harassed you this week?"

"It is, it's complicated. Hudson's dad was killed in the wreck by my late husband. And now his family has moved into the house behind me. It's stirred up the past."

Marty smiled. "So, you've never remarried?"

I laughed, almost falling over my bellows. "No, not me. No one can put up with me. It's just me and my cat."

Marty shrugged his shoulders, not saying another word, and Reed's words announcing Colt came at just the right moment.

Reed said, "We can always use another friend. Today, we have Colt Hinkle from New Boston. He's seven and ready to embark on a possible new talk show for kids. And he's bringing his wisdom to our radio station. So, Colt, say hi to our listeners."

A timid sound came over the speakers. "Hi."

Reed asked, "Well, if there's one thing you'd like folks to know about you, Colt, what would that be?"

"I have a dog. His name is Harry."

"Harry? So, what kind of dog is Harry?"

"The kind that chases cats."

"Like Ms. Beth's cat, Beauty?"

I chuckled under my breath and looked at Marty. "Colt's dog ran my cat up a tree today."

Colt answered Reed. "Yes, he chased her under a storage building and then the tree."

"So what kind is he?"

"He's the chasing kind."

"Well, is he a schnauzer or a bloodhound?"

"Harry's a long-haired chihuahua. He's small. Weighs three pounds."

"So, a dog that's smaller than Ms. Beth's cat can chase her cat?"

"I guess so."

Beep Beep.

Marty nudged me. "There's interference. Did you hear the beeping sound?"

"Yes, I did. It's Colt's insulin pump. I took Colt's phone from my pocket and opened the app that shows his blood sugar. "His sugar is a little high. It beeps when it's low or high. He's supposed to stay within a certain range."

"Should you do something?"

"I'm not sure. This is new for me. I'll text Mindy and see."

Beep. Beep.

Reed looked at the app. "It's high. Not that I know what it should be."

I glanced down. "It has double-arrows up. *Whoa!* I need to call her now."

TREASURES IN BRAVE STEPS

Marty tapped Colt's phone. "It's 231. It's going up. Is that too high?"

"Yes, Mindy just texted me and said to watch it for a bit. If it stays there, Colt will need to adjust with his pump."

I popped into the booth, having jotted a note for Reed telling him what the beep meant. I turned and left as fast as I could, Reed staring at me as if I was interrupting their show.

Reed continued, "So, was that your insulin pump beeping a minute ago?"

"Yes, sir."

"So, is it fine if we talk about juvenile diabetes?"

"I guess so."

"So how long have you had diabetes?"

"A year. I was six when I went to the hospital."

"Did your parents learn about blood sugars with you?"

"At first, they only let my mommy go into the hospital because of the rules. But the next day, Dad got to stay with us because he knew what to do."

"Why does he know what to do?"

"He has diabetes, too. I think he was fourteen when he got sick. He uses insulin pens. I did at first. Then I got the pump."

143

"So how do you feel about having juvenile diabetes?"

I choked, worried Reed had pushed Colt too hard on the topic, his questions overwhelming even me.

Colt answered, "Well, all I know is I'm like my daddy. We know what to do. We know how it feels."

"Does it worry you?"

"I guess it does, well," Colt cleared his throat, "it does when I think about how sick my daddy is."

"Then can you give us some advice?"

"What is… advice?"

"Can you tell people what they should do when life challenges them with diabetes? Or when life gets tough?"

"I guess they should listen for the beep on their pump."

Reed sighed, "Yes, what great advice. When life is pressing in with higher-than-average problems, we might need to adjust and listen for what's beeping for our attention. And when we feel low from the pressures we go through, we could always use a boost, which ultimately comes from God."

Colt sniffled, his nose apparently in need of blowing, the snotty gurgle echoing over the intercom's radio speakers. He responded, "I don't know what you said, but sometimes, I need more insulin. And sometimes I need more carbs."

"Sorry to overthink this, but listeners, if you have a child nearby, have them call Colt with a question. We'll take a five-minute break, and then Colt will be happy to talk to you."

I pressed past Marty to go to Colt and met him in the hallway as he and Reed headed to the back of the building. Reed pointed to a door. "There's the bathroom, buddy. We'll be back on the radio in a few minutes. And blow that nose."

Colt ran to the bathroom, not looking at me, determined and on a mission.

I slapped Reed on the arm. "Seriously, you took Colt down that road? Of all things to talk about, you did that to him?"

"I did what? He has great insight into life, even if it pricks at you and makes you vulnerable. He's a brave kid."

"I know he's brave. But the topic is too much for him."

Marty hovered nearby. "I thought it was good to have such truth coming from such a small child."

Colt bounced into the hallway. "When do I get paid?"

Reed smiled. "You're getting double what we agreed on."

I put my hands on my hips. "And how much did you tell Colt his job pays?"

Reed danced like a tree in the wind, ignoring my question. "Well, we've got a show to finish. Come along, Colt."

Colt tugged on my arm. "I was getting $20. Now I'll get $40."

Reed whispered to Colt, even though Marty and I could hear him. "You're doing great. What will you buy with your money?"

"I'm giving it to Mommy. Daddy's not working, and we need groceries."

With that, the door shut, the light for On-Air shone above the door, and Marty leaned on the wall while I wiped my eyes and hurried to the break room.

Reed's voice took over the building. "Welcome back to our show. This is Reed with KNBO, and today we have a guest. It's our local rising star and talk show host, Colt Hinkle. He may be only seven, but he's ready to tackle your questions. Just give us a call at 903-628-KNBO."

I sat at the table in the break room, processing how my week went from having new neighbors to having their son on the radio. Then I had a revelation as Marty walked into the room. "My word, I never asked Mindy if Colt could speak on air. I already know how Hudson reacted when Mindy and I did our show the other night. I've gone and done it now. They'll never let me babysit again."

Marty assured me. "Just think, he'll help put food on the table. How can that be a bad thing?"

"It's complicated." I put my face into my hands, propping my head up, worrying Mindy might text any moment.

Ring. Ring. Ring.

Reed took the call. "Hello, KNBO. This is Reed and Colt. Talk to us."

A girl's voice spoke. "Hi, this is Holly. Can I talk to Colt?"

"Yes, he's right here. Say hello, Colt."

"Hi." Colt's response was quick.

Holly asked, "Are you the Colt in the choir at church?"

"Yes, I am."

"I was jealous that you got the solo for our back-to-school program. Ms. Beth usually gives me a solo, and I've never had any competition until you started coming to church. I had no idea that you're so brave. And by the way, you sing great. See you Sunday."

Click.

Before Reed could comment about the first call, it ended without Colt's response, and then another call came into the station.

Ring. Ring. Ring.

"Hello, this is KNBO. Talk to us."

"Hi, I'm Lucas. My mom was listening to the radio and heard Colt talking about his insulin pump. She thought I should call. I'm eleven. I found out that I have juvenile diabetes this summer. I don't like the shots."

Reed coughed. "Colt, can you say hi to Lucas and tell him if you were afraid or if you still are?"

A whimper came from deep within Colt. "I'm afraid sometimes. One day last year, I was at school, and I didn't hear the beeping on my pump. A teacher had to carry me from the playground and get me to drink juice. I didn't like how I felt when it went that low."

Tears rolled down my cheeks again, and my insides felt like invisible insulin pens were jabbing at my calloused heart. I shook my head, looking at Marty. "Until you walk with someone, you have no idea what he or she faces."

Marty held back his reaction, cleared his throat four times, and then said, "My father died three years ago. His heart gave out. I was forty-two. I struggled with my faith after he died. It's not that I never believed in God, but when I realized God believed in me, I started to heal and began living again."

I wiped my eyes. "Thank you, now I'm really crying."

Reed piped in, bringing me back to the show, and I knew I'd missed something they'd said.

Lucas asked, "What helps you get through this? I hate being different."

Colt sniffled, his nose running again. "My daddy says we're all different. And we're the same."

Lucas asked, "But we have … we have this disease."

"I know, so maybe this will help a doctor find a cure with so many of us having it."

Reed spoke, "It sounds like you two are the same. You have the same disease. The same hopes. The same fears. But you are facing your journey with courage."

Lucas said, "I'm not brave. I'm not."

Colt remarked, "Me, neither. Unless climbing a tree to save a cat counts as being brave."

Reed added, "Yes, climbing a tree to save a cat will get you a brave badge for sure. So, Lucas, tell me what you have been doing this summer."

"I've played baseball. I'm a pitcher. I ended up in the hospital in Dallas, but once I got regulated, my coach let me come back three days later and pitch in the last game of the tournament."

"Did you win?" Colt asked.

"No, we lost. But I got back on the pitcher's mound."

Reed assured Lucas. "Then, you get a brave badge too. You didn't quit. You went back and played ball."

Reed told Lucas to hold on, that he wanted to get his phone number before he hung up—so Colt and Lucas could arrange to meet.

By the time the recorded weather report finished, I'd used up the rest of the tissues on the table in the break room. "I've cried more this week than I have in years."

Ring. Ring.

The vibration in my pocket told me it was my cell phone. "Hello, Mindy?" I listened to her, then asked if I could put her on speaker since my nose was dripping like a broken faucet.

Mindy went on. "So, a nurse came into the room. She knew our last name. She asked if we had a son. And she asked if his name is Colt."

I added, "And of course, you said yes."

"Yes, I did. That's when she told me about hearing Colt on the radio. Now I argued that wasn't possible, but then again, I knew he was with you—and with you there's no telling what you might do to keep him entertained."

"I just told him we could talk on my show together. I was trying to give him something to do. I'm not good with games, and I'm not sure what to do with a seven-year-old."

"But he's not on your show, is he?"

"No, that's where Reed comes in; they're on the radio right now. They'll be back on the air in about two minutes."

"I know, we've been listening to him. He sounds so shy and so sweet. And by the way, Hudson's stable now, his blood pressure is down, and his headache is gone. Tomorrow, he gets the catheter, and we'll probably be home by Monday. Also, when Colt finishes, give him two units of insulin. His sugar is staying a little high."

"I sure will. So, you're not mad at me?"

"Why would I be mad? Guess who listened to Colt with me? Yeah, Hudson. He cried like a baby when he heard Colt say hi. Who knew that a small hello could do that to a grown man?"

I wiggled in my seat. "Then that means you probably can come back to our show too."

"I can, I'm sure of it. Or I'm pretty sure."

"Wonderful, you have a job with us. I couldn't be happier."

"I'm sure the tide's shifting, and I can take the job."

"I'm beside myself. This is a great day."

"So, how is Colt? He mentioned something about climbing a tree on the show?"

"Oh, that. Harry chased Beauty up the tree. Harry's asleep at my house. And Beauty's stuck in the fort for now."

"Why didn't he get your cat?"

"Well, he sort of fell from the tree."

"Was that when you didn't answer me? His blood sugar dropped about two hours ago, and I couldn't get you."

"Yes, he got dizzy in the tree. But I caught him. And he has a scratch on his arm. He's fine."

Mindy exhaled a long breath over the speakers. "He's my baby boy. He's such a gift. Kiss him for me."

"I'll take good care of him. I promise."

Reed came back on the air. "Hello, listeners, we have time for one more call. But before we take it, do you have a word of wisdom for our listeners?"

Colt answered, "Today I saw my dad's treasures in a shoebox at Ms. Beth's house. She's kept them for twenty years, I think she said."

Reed asked, "Well then, what did you find?"

"I found three cat eye marbles, a barrel of monkeys, and a Rubik's Cube. I also found a viewing thing; I forgot what it's called. You put disks in and watch pictures move by."

"That's probably a View Master."

"Yeah, that's it. And it has stories from Toy Story. I held my dad's Buzz Lightyear, too. He left it in the McDonald's plastic wrapper. But the best part was ... well, it's a secret. I must show him first."

Ring. Ring. Ring.

"Hello, this is Reed at KNBO. Talk to us. You're our final call for today."

The deep voice methodically spoke. "Yes, this is Hudson Hinkle. Is Colt there?"

"Hi, Daddy! Are you coming home? Will you be home in time for supper?"

"Son, I'm better. I'll be here a couple more days, though. But I'll be home soon." Hudson gurgled, his words slowing, his breathing loud.

"Daddy, I'm a star. I'm on the radio."

"I know, that's why I'm calling. A nurse heard you helping another boy who has diabetes. I'm so proud of you."

"Thank you, Daddy. He's the same as me."

"Yes, the same as us."

Reed broke in. "Hello, Hudson. Welcome to your son's debut show. I think he has a huge career in helping others."

"Yes, I think you're right. He's strong. And caring."

Colt put his lips on the mic. "I'm not brave, Daddy, except for trying to save Ms. Beth's cat."

Hudson argued, "You are brave. So, you found my old toys today? And Ms. Beth saved them for me?"

"She did. She said you left your things at her house a lot. I found something else, Daddy. I climbed the tree to your fort. Ms. Beth said you called it a rocket-tree. You left your baseball there."

"A baseball? It's probably ragged by now."

"It's okay. I'll save it forever. It was yours."

Hudson's voice cracked. "Well, tell Ms. Beth we appreciate her. And I ..." his voice went silent, "I love you."

"I love you, Daddy."

Reed wrapped up the call. "Hudson, we know life is hard for you right now. But you're doing a great job with your son. He's the same as you. He's great."

Hudson sighed. "He's different. He's like his mother. Caring and loving."

Colt chimed in, "No, Daddy. I'm like you. I climbed Ms. Beth's tree like you used to. It's the tallest tree in New Boston."

"Son, it was a much smaller tree when I climbed it as a boy."

"But you still climbed it."

Hudson gurgled. "I've got to go. I'm kind of tired. I love you ... Colt Hinkle. Always be brave."

Reed spoke once more, the line still open, but in the background at the hospital, we all heard Mindy's cry, "Hudson, come back. Don't you leave us!"

CAMERA CATCHES ALL

For hours, we've sat at my house today, the longest night behind me, and during my show, Colt slept on a pallet at the station. Now he's moped around mostly—as we all have since we're waiting on word from the hospital.

"Stanley, you should go home. If Mindy calls, I'll let you know how Hudson is doing. He's back with us. Even though it scared us all. So, we're praying for a recovery. And you need your rest."

"I'm here. Let me sit. I'm resting just fine, if you'll let me be."

Gladys shook her head. "Hardheadedness runs in the family. You should know this."

I frowned, and I appreciated being the same as Stanley in that way. "I'm going to sit on the back porch."

Colt shot up from the floor, where he had been stretched out, watching a movie on the iPad. "Can I come outside, too?"

"Sure, let's get some fresh air. That storm last night has cooled everything off. Even Beauty is stretched out on the patio and Harry's asleep by her."

Reed asked, "I'll put lunch in the fridge if everyone's finished."

"Thank you, Reed."

Knock Knock.

Gladys hurried to the door. "I'll get it."

I kept walking with Colt behind me. "Let's go outside and watch for a butterfly."

"Yes, an orange one. Or a yellow one."

Right before I shut the back door, I heard the familiar voice. "Where's my Beth? I need to hug her neck. And I need to do it now."

I rushed back into the living room. "Sally? Sally Snow? I sure need you right now. This week has been the longest ever."

"Well, I'm here now." She greeted Stanley, whose teeth stuck out as if they might fall from his mouth, his eyes shut as he nodded off.

Gladys hugged Sally. "It's been a while. I see you at church, but I haven't made time to be friendly. Time gets away. I'm happy you're here."

"I'm guilty of not being the friend I should be." Sally grabbed my arm. "Let's talk outside."

"That's great. That's where I was headed. Colt's out there now."

We sat in the shade of the porch, while Colt threw a tennis ball against the brick of my house, the end where no windows could get broken.

Sally scratched her nose. "So, what's the latest about Hudson. Is he going to be alright?"

"His heart stopped last night, but he was revived. He's holding his own, but suffered another stroke, and Mindy's worried it will leave him with cognitive issues. She's worried about his memory and concentration. Things like that."

"I hope he finds his way home."

"Yes, Colt's a joy. He's being a trooper; he's not fully aware of what happened last night."

"Poor thing. I lost my mom so young, I never quite got over it, as you know. But having a parent this long … wait, how old is Colt?"

"He's seven."

"Yeah, if Hudson passed away now, that would be so hard on Colt, let alone Mindy."

"I'm struggling to breathe. We sure need some good news."

"Well, I have some good news for you, although this might not be the time to tell you." She held out her left hand with the ring.

"What? No way, you're engaged?"

"Yes, Pearson proposed last week. I wanted to tell you in person, and not on the phone. Will you be my bridesmaid? I'm having a small wedding in the chapel. We're planning it around Christmas."

I hugged her neck hard. "This is great news. You'll make Pearson a great wife. You're like a sister to me. I'm honored you'd ask."

Colt bounded over. "Is that good news about my daddy?"

"Oh, honey, not yet. But I'm sure that call is coming."

Sally spoke, "Hi, Colt. I'm Sally. I heard you're great on the radio."

"I got $40. But I want to see my daddy." Colt ran back to the tennis ball, chunking it a little more complicated than prior tosses.

Sally rose. "I can't stay. Pearson's waiting for me. But I needed to see you and tell you how special you are to me. We're still shopping next week, right?"

"Yes, of course. Life will be back to normal. Surely." I kissed her engagement ring. "You'll be the prettiest bride ever. Will Ruby Nell make it in for the wedding?"

"She might. Her art show closes out in New York at the end of November."

"See you next week. Congratulations. I love you."

Sally disappeared inside, leaving the backyard to Colt and me, and my phone sat on the patio table. I tapped it to check the time. "Colt, we have a few hours until I go to the station. I thought I'd be off for the weekend, but keeping busy helps me stay busy. Stanley and Gladys offered to stay here with you. Would you like that?"

"No, I want to go where you go. I'll take my earbuds and iPad and stay on the blanket next to you."

"That sounds like a plan. We have choir practice on Sunday night at six. So, you might go over your song, too."

"I know it backwards and forwards. When's our program?"

"It's in two weeks. I'm sure your dad will be home in time."

Colt threw the ball. "I hope so."

I sighed under my breath and flipped through my phone apps, jumping to my email, then to Facebook, then to checking my bank balance.

I tapped on the camera app for snippets of recordings from the week at my house. When I saw one I'd missed, I'd tap it.

Most of the time, I wished I'd never placed those cameras on the side of my house, in the back of my home, and along the fence row by the street. They were originally there to let me see if the skunks were out or the raccoons were hunting for food in my trash.

I enlarged the recording, turning the phone sideways to get a better look. "Who is that in my yard? And what is he doing?"

The visitor was human, and with his movements, he was trying to make a point. It was Hudson right before the first phone call to the station when he yelled at me.

I pulled my phone closer, and thanks to my camera, I captured every move Hudson made, every moment of his marching across my yard. I had a video of every step he took. I leaned in, the sound low on my phone.

Hudson cried when he touched the tree by the bird feeder. I hated having to watch such a video, but I couldn't quit. But I'm not sure what to do with the information because now I know he trespassed the night my door was open—even though I'd left it unlocked.

I whispered, "Wait, there he is. He's opening the back door, all three locks. He knew where I kept the spare key, too. He found it on the ledge in the storage building. Why didn't I think of that? But wait, he didn't go inside. He started to, but didn't."

I glanced over at Colt, who chased, raced, and played wall ball. Then I looked at his sleeping dog, Harry, and my contented cat. Hudson's challenges are greater than any I've imagined. Just think, if I'd had him arrested for harassment the other night, he would be in jail with more problems. I'm thankful I didn't go down that road.

I squinted, trying to see what Hudson did next. "What's he looking at?" I watched as he stood there, and he lingered, his shoulders shaking uncontrollably. "He's remembering. He's remembering good days in the yard, playing in the fort, playing in the water."

I whispered to the cool breeze. "I'm deleting this for good. It's never to be seen. I don't need to have this on here."

Beauty meowed, her green eyes squinting as if she agreed. It's not like I haven't forgiven my cat for the times she knocked milk from my hand. Or had an accident on the floor.

It's not like I haven't forgiven Sally or Stanley or even Reed. Sometimes, the children will test me in choir, but I always forgive them. So, I should forgive Hudson—he's in a rough place.

Meow. Meow.

I drifted in and out of memories from last week. The hardest thing for me to give away is mercy. It's the opposite of how I feel. Forgiveness is offered to us by Jesus, and often I forget to practice His ways. I think I've got a right to hold a grudge. And then I do, and I bury it. Only to remember it time and again.

But when I consider Jesus, I pray that He gives me the strength to do the impossible. I rewound the video, watching it one more time, knowing that if I didn't hit Delete, I'd let the prison of my past open like a video on replay.

I prayed, "Lord, show me how. Please show me how to do this. Let me set someone else free from the shackles of his past. Please."

Colt charged up to me. "What are you watching? Is it a movie?"

"Oh, it's just an old recording from those cameras on my house."

"Can I watch one?"

"Oh, we've got much better things to do." I hit Delete and the video swept away to a land of forgiveness—where sin goes to die—to where old videos disappear.

"Do you know where I put my daddy's baseball?"

"Yes, it's with the shoebox. You put it inside so that we wouldn't lose it."

I followed Colt into the kitchen, my smile giving me away, and Reed asked from the sink. "What have you been up to?"

"I'm doing the right thing. In the past, I've chosen the upper hand instead of practicing with an open hand."

"What? You're talking in riddles like me now?"

I smirked. "I've been around you way too long. Why did I wait so long to unlock the doors of my past? To release the others who got inside my cell?"

Reed's nostrils flared. "Who is in your cell?"

157

"There's the woman who is jealous of those who have great families. The woman who is afraid she'll suffocate from the pain. The woman has regrets for how she treated her foster parents. The woman who judged another hurting soul. The woman who held grudges. Who fought to make a point. The woman who was in bondage to a terrible, abusive marriage."

Reed nodded. "It sounds pretty crowded in that jail cell."

"Not anymore. The chains are breaking off. The locks are open. The gate is wide open. The fence will come down. Freedom is upon us."

"You're taking down your fence?"

I contemplated the idea. "Yes, I don't want the fence. I need to be free. I'll use the money to fix my car and hire someone to put a lock on each door in the house. And I'll hire that man down the street to take the fence down. To build a new rocket fort too."

"Let me fix your car. You do need a reliable ride."

"You've done so much for me already."

"It's just money. Let me be free with it."

I marched around the breakfast bar, hugging Reed, whose wrinkles were less droopy than Stanley's, but still there, nonetheless. "Thank you for being such a great friend."

"You're welcome." Reed lifted my chin. "I watched you out the kitchen window. I could tell you had a recording of someone on your security system. Was it Hudson?"

"It was him. I didn't see this recording the other night, but he was here. It was the same night when I found my front door open. He knew where I hid my extra key. I guess I should have picked another spot, but I never expected to see him again."

"And you deleted the video, didn't you?"

"Yes, it was time to get rid of such things from my life."

"And how freeing is that?"

"I feel like I could fly."

Reed smiled. "I expect you feel like you could sing too."

I nodded, "I may surprise you real soon. Singing is something I've been considering off and on this week."

Reed called to me as I left the kitchen. "I speak the name of Jesus over you and your walk. I pray for your heart to heal, and for circumstances to change. I pray for continued breakthroughs and for miracles in this house."

I stopped walking, turning back to face Reed, and Colt ran up, taking my hand.

Reed continued, "I pray the power of Christ restores health to Colt's father. That the God who knows we're facing the impossible makes all things new. May He use the talk show to speak life into this community. I pray for Holly, David, and their family. For Lucas. For Sally and Pearson's marriage."

I put my hand up. "You know about Sally?"

"Yes, Pearson told me."

Stanley readied to continue the prayer, standing next to Colt, holding his hand, while Gladys took her husband's hand. Then someone else came alongside us. The man took mine. I turned my head. "Marty? When did you get here?"

"I've been here for close to an hour. I slipped in when you were in the back and you've been distracted, so I just sat in the recliner minding my own business until I could stand with you in agreement that we're seeking God for direction."

I squeezed his hand. "I'm glad you came. I'm a terrible hostess."

Colt changed the subject. "I thought we were praying."

Reed closed our circle, placing himself between Marty and Gladys, while Stanley moved on in prayer. "Dear Lord, on behalf of Colt Hinkle, we pray for his dad to come home. We pray for the past to leave and that no memory of the loss will haunt him. May our hearts tell a story of hope and sing a song of how You, Jesus, cared for us through these years."

Colt added when Stanley took a deep breath. "And Jesus, can Ms. Beth sing with me in the program. Please?"

Marty squeezed my hand, and I thought the lump in my throat might cause me to suffocate. I winked at Colt. "We'll see how it comes together. We'll see."

Buzz. Buzz. Buzz.

The phone call we hoped for came, but would the message be the answer we longed for? I clutched my cell, handed it to Marty, who passed it to Stanley, who gave it to Gladys, who shoved it into Reed's hand.

Reed answered, "Yes, no, this isn't Beth. This is her secretary from the radio station, Reed Rider."

I frowned. "Is it Mindy?"

Reed listened to the caller but didn't answer me. "Yes, I'll tell her. And yes, Colt is right here; he's stepping on my toes in hopes he can talk to you."

Reed handed Colt the phone. "Hi, Mommy." He paused. "Yes, really? He's awake. He's coming home Monday?"

Colt wept, dropping my phone on the tile—the exact spot where Stanley plowed to the floor in the kitchen when Beauty caused him to stumble.

I picked up the phone. "Mindy, are you there? This is great news, just great." I paused. The words she said next sent me to my knees.

"Beth, I'm worried about how much time we have left with Hudson. His body just keeps breaking down."

I uttered, "Just remember, one step at a time. All we can do is take a breath and find hope in the present. Remember, God is our strength. In all things."

LIFE IS LIKE MONOPOLY

Sunday night, choir practice went as one might expect, and I felt like I was herding sheep rather than children. Now, I'm on the couch, while Colt is kicked back asleep in the recliner. All day, his joy spilled over like someone had shaken him up like a carbonated soda pop. He kept exploding with energy. And he was into everything, talking too much, and beyond busy with activity.

Oh, to watch his joy bubble over made me shout with praise at how God works all things for good to those who believe— even though most of the good we'll ever experience will come much later in Heaven.

Colt begged me to sing with him, but I gave the duet to Holly instead so that she could sing with him. I'll do the closing chorus with them. "Amazing Grace" will never be the same when we finish singing for the congregation, nor the other three songs that the two children's choirs will attempt from memory.

It's only eight and I can barely stay awake. Mindy's driving home to change out Colt's cartridge on his pump and to change his Dexcom, since that isn't something I know how to do yet. But so far, Colt has educated me on how to adjust his insulin even before Mindy sends me a text.

Harry is snuggled up next to me, as if he were happy moving into my house. I rubbed his ear, and he pressed closer to my leg. As for Beauty, she's tolerating Harry, but not without hissing at him periodically.

I made a few phone calls today; the fence comes down next week. The locks are changed out on the front and back doors, too—one deadbolt on each. And by next weekend, there will be a new fort in the tree—but not in my yard. It's a surprise for Colt; he has several oaks towering behind his house. A rocket fort will be in his, ready for climbing and imaginary trips where he can look for butterflies.

The baseball is missing, and we've searched for it and turned up nothing. We couldn't find it yesterday, either, after Stanley and Gladys went home. That's the only time Colt's cried, whenever he thought about the old, worn-out ball and how it's gone. I was sure we put it into the shoebox, and I have no clue as to what we've done with it—or where it's hiding.

Tap. Tap.

I shuffled to the back door, opening the latch. "Mindy! What a great way to end the weekend. Oh my, you look exhausted." I hung on her neck, my arms embracing one of the bravest souls I'm privileged to know.

Mindy collapsed into my arms. "I need my bed and my own pillow, that's for sure. Hudson is doing better than we could have imagined, too. He's not thrilled about the catheter, but the journey of his dialysis treatment begins. He'll start that soon and go to Texarkana for training. Then his supplies will come. Then he'll do his treatment at home for eight hours each night."

"Oh wow. And to think I get trapped in worrying over small things, when Hudson's going through so many difficult seasons." I wiped a tear, gathering my thoughts. "Yesterday, I said we needed some good news. And I know you did too —

look at how Hudson is responding. That's great news! I'm so happy to hear your voice, to see you."

A padding sound on the floor came our way. "Mommy!" Colt latched onto Mindy as he might never let go.

"Honey, let's go to the house. I'll switch out your cartridge and Dexcom. We'll sit and talk for a while. It seems I have a famous son now." She kissed his blond hair no less than six times, and Colt held Mindy's hand as if they would remain connected for life.

"I'm not famous. I just talked to people." Colt's wrinkled brow was a sign that he had no idea the impact he made with Reed on the radio.

"Let's go home. But wait, where's Harry?"

Colt pointed. "He's asleep in the living room. He likes it here."

Mindy smiled. "I think you like it here, too."

"I do, but I love being with you and Daddy better."

Mindy and Colt slipped onto the patio, heading to the gate, while I imagined the backyard open and without a fence.

Yawning, I moved to the couch, where Harry slept, and where I planned to curl up and rest until Colt returned. I nodded off, half awake and half asleep, my foot twitching, my hands tingling with exhaustion.

Behind my eyes, the waterfall from the dream I experienced earlier in the week with the rushing river returned. But instead of holding a bucket and trying to empty the river of water, I splashed by the shoreline, laughing like a girl of twenty. And down the riverbank, Hudson was ten and dancing on the rocks, playing like a small boy, like the one I met so long ago.

He smiled and looked my way, running into my arms, and his whisper came, "I don't blame you. I know you've suffered too."

I jerked awake, crying like a baby. "Lord, let the dream come true and let it become the new truth in my relationship with Hudson." My sobs stirred Harry and brought Beauty to the headrest behind me, where she rubbed her head on my ear. I reached for her, cradling her in my arms while Harry's nose twitched, and he sniffed her paw.

**

The peace of that moment shifted when Colt stormed into the living room from the kitchen. "I'm back! Mommy's coming with my PJs. She had me take my shower too and brush my teeth." He pounced on my lap, scattering Harry to the floor and sending Beauty scampering to the other end of the couch.

I rustled his hair. "You smell like soap. Much better. Did you wash behind your ears?"

"I poured shampoo over me. I just let the water run so I can get clean. But Mommy made sure I washed my hair. I forget, sometimes."

Mindy lit up the room with her smile. "Phew, we'll be home tomorrow, but I'm on my way back to the hospital. Colt, be good and don't keep Beth up. Her eyes are red, and she's not used to having someone underfoot."

"He's no trouble. He's brought my little brick house to life. It's been quiet for too long. Do you need anything from me? Do I need to do anything at your house?"

"No, you've done so much for us. I can't thank you enough for being Colt's choir director and now, our neighbor. God knew we needed to be right in this cul-de-sac for Hudson to face his past and to heal, and for me to find a friend."

I felt my throat tightening. "I'm pretty sure it was long overdue for me, too. I avoided Hudson at all costs for years. It's been a rough week, but things are looking up."

Mindy nodded. "Well, I hope you're right. Walking free and living with hope has eluded our little family. It's time we unlock the joy the Lord has for us—to embrace the mercy God's offered us too."

I walked with Mindy to the back door. "Text me when you get to the hospital."

"I will." She moved around me to Colt. "Give me a hug. And be good," she said, wrapping her arms around his neck.

"I'll be good."

"Your dad and I'll be home sometime tomorrow. Love you, buddy." Mindy hurried out the door, with streams of tears gushing like a waterfall.

I cracked the door open, calling to her over the fence. "Be careful. And I can't wait to work on our radio show together."

Her voice trailed. "I'll be back before you know it."

Inside, Colt asked me to play a game, one he'd brought with him from his house earlier in the day, after we went for Harry's dog food. He held up a box. "Do you want to play Toy Story Monopoly?"

"Well, I see you brought Bingo too. That's fun."

Colt grabbed a box and placed it on the coffee table. "I like Monopoly. I'll set it up, and I'm going to be Buzz Lightyear. Who do you want to be?"

I dug in the box, moving the silver images around. "I'll be Andy. He's a cool toy."

"I'll be the banker."

We sorted out the money to start the game while Beauty spied our maze of possible items to attack from the edge of the couch. "Beauty don't mess with this game. These are not your toys."

165

Colt giggled, "She's going to jump. I bet she will."

I shook my head. "Beauty's a good cat, most of the time." I motioned to the stack of money. "You're in charge of making change for us, too."

We rolled the two dice to see who went first. Colt laughed, "I rolled ten. You only had four. I'll go first."

He rolled the one die, moving ahead five spots to the Claw, drawing a card, and collecting $50 for rescuing some character I'd never heard of before."

I tossed my die, moved Woody to the spot where I landed, and got to roll again. Then I ended up in the place where I visited the jail on the corner of the board. "It's a good thing I'm just visiting."

"Mommy said you could have sent Daddy to jail, but that you showed us grace." He paused. "What is grace?"

"I guess it's showing goodness to someone who might not deserve it," I explained, grace in a simple phrase, not wanting to overcomplicate the situation.

"Mommy shows me grace then. Sometimes she said I deserve to be punished for riding my hoverboard in the house. But so far, she just takes it away for a day or so."

"You have a hoverboard?"

"Yes, my Aunt Melody got it for me. She sends me good presents for my birthday."

"Well, you have a mommy who is kind too. I'm glad to get to know her and to meet you finally."

We tossed the die, laughed about buying property, and I got tickled at how Colt loved to exchange his twenties for larger bills. I tried to show him how to count change, starting with the correct rent and working up to the money in his hand.

Colt nudged me, grinning. "Don't make me do math. I'm on summer break. We do math in school."

"But this whole game is about math. There are houses to buy—hotels to get. Rent to pay. That involves math."

Colt argued, "No, it's a game. Math happens at school."

I chuckled, "You're so right! What was I thinking?"

For the next two hours and a hundred yawns later, I lost the game after mortgaging my properties, and even after Colt gave me his money to try to keep me from losing.

I hugged Colt. "We've got to get some sleep. You're great at this."

He grinned. "It's because I'm good at math."

"And so, you are."

"First, we must pick this all up. Mommy says if you put the game up right, then it's ready for the next time."

I blew a whistle of tiredness. "Then let's pack it up."

I suspect Beauty thought her chance to grab a game piece was about to end, and she pounced onto the board game. We scrambled for flying property cards, for Treasure Chest and Claw cards, and then fell to our backs on the floor with play money littered around us as if we were rich.

I tickled Colt. "Is this how we put up the game?"

He rolled his eyes. "It's the long way."

I tossed up a handful of ones. "It's the best way!"

With the last piece of Monopoly money in the box, I glanced at the time on my phone. "It's almost eleven. Bed, we're going to bed."

Colt asked, "Can I play five minutes on the iPad?"

"Yes, then it's to bed. It's a good thing it's summer."

Colt offered me a sheepish grin.

I tapped my text app, wondering why Mindy hadn't sent me her note that she'd arrived at the hospital. I texted: Goodnight. See you tomorrow."

I then noticed I had a text from an unknown number. Not one. Not two. But three texts. It read: This is Hudson. Where's Mindy?"

THE GREAT ESCAPE

Most of the night I spent every anxious moment trying not to fall asleep. I had texted Marty to see if he might go to the hospital and see if Mindy's SUV was in the parking lot, since he lives in Texarkana.

Fortunately, he was kinder than I would be to someone waking me up from a sound sleep. He scoured the lot and drove the interstate, only to see a stranded SUV on the side of the Eastbound, and he made the next exit, where he discovered Mindy. Her cell phone was dead, her charger was at the hospital, and she was distraught. Her tire on the passenger side was also flat.

Thanks to Marty, he changed her tire and got her moving, while I texted Hudson, keeping him posted. Throughout the next two hours, Colt slept on the couch next to the iPad, with Harry at his feet and Beauty on his side.

Apparently, the game of Monopoly continued, and was in full gear, where life unfolds, where the dice give you answers you don't want, where you dream of having enough money for new tires. Still, you barely have enough money for groceries and gas for your vehicle.

I kissed Colt on the head. "Thank you for thinking of your mother when Reed gave you the $40. Never lose your compassion, sweet boy."

I crumpled next to the couch, my legs tired, my eyes burning from the layers of the past week. Tomorrow's a new day, and it awaits. Dialysis will keep a man alive. A small boy will monitor his insulin. And soon we'll perform our back-to-school program.

I hope, in some small way, to teach the youth to praise God with all their might, no matter what flattens out their hope. May they run to Jesus with their cares and not let tragedy take away their ability to believe God is with them through all things.

**

Beep. Buzz. Beep.

I stirred from a deep sleep, and the noise sent me to my feet. "What time is it? Wait, is that your pump, Colt? Or the doorbell? Or my phone?" I spun around half-asleep, my legs numb from sitting on the floor, sleeping with my head on a cushion. "Wait, it's light in here. How long did I sleep?"

I glanced at the sofa. "Colt, where are you?"

A faint voice called from the hallway. "I'm in the bathroom."

"Is your sugar low?"

"No, ma'am."

I stood outside the bathroom door. "Are you sure?"

"I'm sure."

Buzz. Buzz. Buzz. Ding.

"That's my phone. Someone's texting me and calling." I charged to the living room, digging for my phone under the recliner where the buzzing continued. "There! I've got it! It's

Mindy. She left me a voicemail and texted me, too. Oh good, she and Hudson are on their way home early and will be here by ..." I looked at the time on the screen. "By nine this morning? They're home or should be. It's almost ten."

I charged down the hall again, shouting through the door. "Are you sure your blood sugar isn't low?"

"I'm fine," Colt assured me.

In minutes, he surfaced, shuffling to my side. "You slept a long time. I found some Nutella and pretzels. It has 36 calories, and I took my insulin."

"So, that was your breakfast?"

"Yeah, and it was the best. Mommy never has Nutella for breakfast!"

"Good, I hope she won't mind." I sighed, relieved that no other crisis scenarios unfolded while I slept like a pretzel. I touched Colt's shoulder. "Well, we have good news. Your dad and mom should be at the house by now. Let's walk over."

Colt grabbed the shoebox. "I can't wait to show Daddy all his things you saved. But I wish we could find the baseball."

"It's not lost. We had it. It will show up."

I traipsed with Colt down the fence along the curb with Harry on our heels. "Thank you for staying with me. I hope you weren't bored."

"No, you're not too boring." Colt scampered beneath the carport next to his mom's SUV and disappeared inside right after waving to me—while clutching his box of treasures.

As I marched home, I turned on my water sprinklers —one on the side, one in the backyard —and then ended up at the front, twisting the faucet by the front porch.

A red Jeep rounded the corner up the street, turning in front of my house, where the driver stopped and parked. I moved to the passenger door as the window went down. I ran my fingers through my tangled hair, putting it behind my ears, and wiped the crust from my eyes. "Marty? What brings you here?"

"I'm headed to the station, and thought I'd check on you."

"I don't need anyone checking on me." I found myself wishing to take back my response.

Marty held the steering wheel. "We all need help from time to time. I'm thankful I found Mindy safely parked on the interstate last night. But she was quite the ..." Marty contemplated his choice of words.

I finished his sentence. "She was quite the wreck?"

"Yes, for lack of a better description. But she calmed down after she realized I wasn't going to hurt her and that you'd sent me. I ordered her four new tires this morning at J&G Tires on Highway 8. When they come in, she can go have the tires put on."

"That was kind of you. She'll be so grateful." I smiled. "Did you tell her?"

"No, that's another reason I'm here. You can be my messenger. No need to tell her who paid for them." Marty tapped the wheel. "Well, I'd better go. There's work at the station waiting for me. I'll see you later."

"Um, sure. I'll be in at five. And don't do all my recordings. I love taping them."

"Sure thing, since you don't need anyone helping you." He snickered, as if mocking me.

"You might get in trouble for making fun of me. Most people don't like coffee grounds in their coffee."

"I don't drink coffee too much. I'm more of a mango tea drinker, myself."

"You are not. I drink mango tea, and you know that."

"You're not the only person who can like flavored tea." And with that, Marty revved the engine, put the Jeep in drive, and waved. "See you at work." And he drove away.

I blushed, not from the sun, but because I'd had a conversation with someone my own age—and it didn't come with chaos. "I've almost forgotten how to talk to people in person. I'm used to having a microphone."

The sprinkler shot its spray at me as the wind picked up, as the fluffy white clouds rolled in, as the shade of a new day felt like spring instead of summer.

**

So far tonight, some thirteen calls have come into the station, with people asking about Mindy, others praying for her return, and a few filtering through with nosy questions about Hudson. Fifteen minutes before midnight, and now the phone is ringing. "Hello, Beth Bender. Bend my ear. It's late. What's on your mind?"

"Hi, I waited until he fell asleep. He works in construction and drinks all day. He keeps guzzling his beers until he can't function. He reeks of booze, slobbers when he talks, and if I get too close, he hits me until I run off and lock myself in the bathroom."

"Your husband?"

"Yes, but he's not much of one."

I asked, "Are you in the bathroom now?"

"I am, but I know he's asleep in his chair. That's how many of our nights end. He'll wake up in the morning and act like nothing happened."

"Can you go somewhere right now?"

"I don't have anywhere to go."

173

Marty and Reed appeared in the window outside my booth, listening and staring at me. They'd stay late to work out scheduling and go through Stanley's books, since he's not great with finances.

I waved them off, not happy, and they glared at me as if I were in jail in a game of Monopoly. But they didn't leave.

The woman cried. "I should go. This is a bad idea."

"No, wait. So, how long have you been married? And what did you say your name was?"

"I didn't say my name. I can't. My husband's known in town. His family is from Bowie County. He has brothers and sisters, aunts, and uncles who all live within range of your station. No one knows that side of him. I can't ruin his reputation."

"But he's hurting you. And you're hiding in a bathroom even as he sleeps."

"I know, it doesn't make sense. But he's hit me since we dated in high school. It's gone on for ten years." She wept harder when she said the word *ten* as if she realized how long the suffering had lasted.

"Let me come and pick you up."

"Pick me up?"

"Yes, I get off in a minute. The show's about to end, let me come over. Then you can have a restful night at a hotel where you'll sleep, and then we can talk in the morning."

Reed and Marty shook their heads. It's like they wanted to warn me that I'd gone too far with my offering of help. But hey, without my helping her now, tomorrow might not come.

"Beth, are you there?"

"I'm still here. Can you tell me how it started?"

"Oh my, how did it start?"

"When did he start hitting you?"

"In high school. He slapped me, then punched me. Once, we were at a movie. I'd talked him into taking me to a girl flick, *The Help,* and he asked for popcorn and a Coke, and even a hot dog. He waited until the movie started, and I teased him about why he didn't ask for snacks during the previews. Then he slammed his fist into my jaw. We were in the last row in the theater, and no one saw anything."

"I'm so sorry! How horrible for you."

"I was terrified and took his money, stormed to the snack bar, and left the theater, walking the seven miles home. That wasn't the only time, once he left me unconscious in the road by his parents' house. Another time, he hit me in front of our Algebra teacher. When I tried to get away, he apologized and promised not to hit me again."

"But it continued, didn't it?"

"Yes, now I'm pretty much stuck here. He gets the groceries. I don't buy my own clothes. It's like I'm in a jail cell with no get-out-of-jail card."

"I'm picking you up. Pack yourself a bag. We'll take you to the hotel. I'll reach out to someone at the local domestic violence center in the morning. Please, let me come for you?"

"You can come. But somehow, he'll find me, and when he does, I'd wish I never called the radio station."

"No, this must stop. You are precious in God's sight. Don't hang up. I'll get your address as soon as I close out the show. Five minutes. Hold on."

I tied a knot on the closing segment of my show, playing a recorded devotional. I then went back to the call, making sure the woman was there—but as soon as I spoke, she countered, "I'm fine. This was a mistake. I can't give you my address."

I fumbled for words. "Wait, my husband hit me, too. The last day I saw him alive, he had held me up against our bedroom wall, his hands on my neck. You must let me help you. God put you in my path for this moment. Please?"

The woman's sobs were low. "If he finds me, he'll kill me."

"If you stay, he could kill you." I spouted those words before I could inhale or exhale. Reed and Marty hovered next to me—but gave me my space—I was on a mission for God, an assignment I'd never asked for.

"My address is ..." she whispered the numbers to me, and I almost fell out of my chair.

I put my hand on the receiver, speaking to Reed and Marty, who had joined me. "It's my neighbor up the street. He's the man I hired to take down my fence and to build Colt's fort. Well, so much for that, he's fired."

I got back to the woman and promised her. "I'll be right there. Ten minutes. Be ready. I'm driving an old truck; my car is in the shop."

The woman whimpered a bit, but said she'd wait for me in her yard. I gasped, hanging up the receiver, and Marty put his hand on my shoulder. "Are you okay?"

"I will be. I must be. Just pray that I can give hope to this woman—that she'll let me put her up for the night."

Marty nodded, and Reed agreed with him. "We'll follow you, if that's okay. If her husband happened to wake up, things might not go well."

Marty assured me. "I'll tag along and park up the street. Reed, this will raise your blood pressure. So go home. We'll let you know how it went in the morning."

"I'm old, but ..." Reed paused, "Fine, I'll go home. If you need the police, please do call them."

I assured Reed. "I will. But I must do for her what I might not have ever done for myself—if Rhett had lived."

At her house, the shadows hung low, the night dark except for streetlights lining the houses. I parked, waiting for a minute, and rolled the passenger window down. About three houses behind me, a Jeep was parked too, waiting with me, helping me do the right thing for this woman.

The door swung open, and a bloody-faced woman slid into my car. She cried, "Drive on. Hurry, before he wakes up."

I inched along, not turning on my lights. "There's a gash by your cheekbone. You need a doctor."

"I'll bandage it at the hotel. I can't go to the hospital. He'll find me."

"Are you sure?"

"I am. Just drive." The woman clutched a small bag, her hands covered in blood, her wrists bruised with last week's injuries. And silence fell inside the truck, except for her sobs.

The woman sniffled. "We've been driving for an hour. Where's this hotel?"

"It's in another county. I don't want your husband to find you. We're almost there. Do you have any family? A mother or father you can stay with? Or shall I go ahead and call Domestic Violence in the morning?"

"If I go to my mother's house, he'll find me. I can't go there."

"We'll take this one day at a time. It's time for you to find peace and live without this pain."

"I hope you're right."

The next hour, Marty and I checked her into the hotel, an old place from back in time—but the bed was clean. The man at the counter thought Marty and I were a couple, so that worked out great. No suspicion from the hotel clerk to alert anyone of a woman hiding in a hotel room."

Right before I shut the door, I asked, "Do you need anything? Anything at all?"

"I'm worn out. I haven't slept in years. So, you'll come for me in the morning?"

"I will, right about ten. Then we'll make some plans."

"Thank you," her voice quivered. "I can't believe I called the talk show tonight. I've considered calling for the past two years."

"You've listened to my ramblings that long?"

"I have. You always give me hope at night when I can't sleep. Always."

I hugged the woman, a small, petite blonde, and it was as if I stood staring into a mirror, and I saw myself from twenty years ago. "Get some sleep. Your new life awaits."

Beside my car, I wept like a baby, sobbing uncontrollably. Marty scooted up next to me. "Would it be all right if I held you?"

I didn't answer, and embraced Marty, soaking his shirt with a thousand tears—each drop filled with guilt from a wreck I had no control over. "I'm free. I'm finally free."

Marty asked, "Free from what?"

I moved away, wiping snot from his shoulder. "I've carried a burden I wasn't meant to carry. I'm not doing that anymore. I'm free to be me."

"But how will we help that lady? Won't she be prone to go back?"

I pursed my lips. "She will be."

"How do you know?"

"Because I was married for only two years, left five times, and always went back. Leaving is harder than staying. The fear of the repercussions kept me in bondage. I can only pray the Lord has set her steps into motion—to where she finds freedom."

RACCOONS AFTER DARK

I yawned. It's Tuesday afternoon, and already the morning is a blur of connecting dots and activity. A door opened that I didn't expect, which helped the woman at the hotel, because she phoned her cousin in Arizona and flew out of Texarkana right after lunch. The relative is a cousin of a cousin on her mother's side, one never mentioned by most of the family.

So, the secret escape was off and running —literally taking off from an airport runway — and my excitement for my late-night caller was filled with more tears that fell like spring rain.

I held Beauty to my chest while drinking mango tea on my back porch. "Girl, I wish I had nine more lives. I feel like I've used mine up this week."

Meow. Meow.

I kissed her head. "Girl, I canceled my fence demolition and fort-building contract. Can you believe it? When I talked with him, he didn't say one word about his wife's disappearance. That's a good sign, it's not like he knows me very well, or vice versa."

I took a sip of tea. "Beauty, I like that, Marty. He's a kind soul, and he's hired someone else to take down my fence and to build the fort. Mindy plans to come to work tonight, too. I'm so thrilled." I licked my lips. A mixture of cat hair and sweet tea made a gooey blob on my tongue. "Yuck! That's nasty!"

Reed's taking the day off. Hudson is on the mend as best as he can be, considering his kidney disease and diabetes complications. Stanley's giving out orders again, so Gladys is baking to get away from Captain Stanley. And Colt is on his way over to play in the water sprinkler. From what I've heard, I'll get my Accord back from the shop this Friday.

"Hi Colt, it's time to cool off, isn't it?"

"Yes, ma'am."

I held up a brown baseball. "Look what I found."

"Where did you find it?"

"It was under the recliner. I saw a piece of Monopoly money on the floor, and then I saw the ball right beside it. See, it wasn't lost, the ball was just hiding from us."

Colt clutched the ball. "Sorry, I can't play now. I must show my daddy. I must give him his ball. Then he'll know."

"He'll know what?"

"That certain things aren't lost forever. They can show up any time."

Colt left the yard, the sprinkler casting its arch of water back and forth, and for a few minutes, I pondered the depth of Colt's words. I announced to Beauty, "Weeping may last for the night, but a shout of joy comes in the morning. Or in my case, in the afternoon."

The squeak from the gate made me look up. "Colt, did you forget something?"

"No, it's me, Marty. I thought I'd stop by to check on you."

"That's twice you've checked on me. I'm fine."

"Can I join you for some mango tea?"

"Seriously, you don't drink mango tea."

Marty plopped into the chair across from me. "I may drink mango tea, if you'll pour me some." He smiled, as if he was not really interested in tea.

"Sure, I'll get you a glass. It's sweet."

"Sounds great."

As Marty and I sat in the shade, I revisited my thoughts about what Colt said regarding things not being lost forever. "Hey Marty, in the Psalms, David experienced many ups and downs throughout his life. He was not a stranger to sorrow, yet he still had many victories. He always cried out to God when life got tough, even in his frustrations. And David lifted his voice in praise to God, too."

Marty sipped his tea, slurping like a kid. "Are you going somewhere with this?"

"Yes, it's time for me to sing at church again. I've led the children's choirs, but stopped singing in service after Rhett died, after Hudson's dad died. Instead, I taught others to sing, but I have a voice too. It's time for me to do my part."

"So, your singing isn't lost?"

"Were you at the gate when Colt left?"

"Yes, I heard him say certain things aren't lost forever."

"You are the nosey one."

"Excuse me, I think you're the one who is nosey."

"Whatever, but I believe God is calling me to sing again. What do you think?"

"So, you want my advice?'

"Sure, it's not like you don't have an opinion."

"Then you must sing. And you must go out on a date with me."

"Oh, my goodness. One glass of tea doesn't mean I'll go out with you."

"Fine then, I'll ask someone else."

"Wait, who would that be?"

"Why do you care?" Marty smirked and gulped the rest of his tea down. "This tea is terrible. Too sweet. Too much mango."

"It's mango tea. What did you expect?'

"I don't know, I just came by ..."

"I know, you came by to check on me."

"So, will you let me take you on a date?"

"Maybe, I'll think about it."

**

I hugged Mindy after a near-perfect night on the radio, with calls, laughter, and hope planted in our listeners' hearts. "Mindy, I can't imagine you not being on the radio. You are destined to do this. Thank you for being here."

"I'm thrilled to find something I'm good at, and the encouragement you give to those who call in; well, it's for me too. I've felt myself looking ahead lately. I'm thankful for this station and for you and for this town."

"So, Hudson was fine with Colt staying home tonight?"

"Yes, he didn't mind at all. He said there was no reason to keep Colt up so late." Mindy touched her back pocket. "Wait, that's my phone. Yes, what is it, Colt?" She paused. "I'll be there in a second. No, I didn't run away. I'm working with Beth, remember?"

I unloaded my questions. "Is everything okay? Does Hudson need something? Is Colt's blood sugar okay?" I hovered close; my nosiness was evident, and I guess Marty was right about that part of my personality.

"Yes, all is well. Colt got up, went to the bathroom, and couldn't find me. So, he got scared."

"Good, you know he's singing at the church with Holly in less than two weeks."

"I know. Colt told me. He said her brother's arm was broken too."

"Yes, but David likes his cast and had everyone sign it. And thankfully, they're staying with their grandmother along with their mom."

Mindy scratched her nose. "You never know what people are facing behind closed doors."

I sighed, "That's so right."

I touched her hand and held it. "My door is always open. So that you know."

"Thank you. It's nice to have a friend."

We embraced like sisters from different mothers, but with the same God, our Father. I smiled. "Let's go home."

I no sooner got out of Stanley's truck than Mindy charged to the house. "I can't find them."

I stomped to the side of the house as we rushed to her driveway. "What do you mean, you can't find them?"

"I went inside, and the kitchen light was on. I picked up Harry from the chair next to the couch and went to check on Colt. His bed was empty. So, I figured he'd gotten into my bed and was sleeping with Hudson. But they're both gone."

"No way, that can't be true."

We marched into her house, to the kitchen, and she turned on all the lights. "What are we going to do? Hudson's irrational behavior is pushing me over the top."

"There's got to be a logical reason. But wait, his car is gone."

"It's at Stanley's house from the other day. Stanley didn't have a car to drive since you have his truck."

"But he has Gladys' car."

183

"She needed her car to work at the church for the back-to-school program."

I sighed, "Keeping up with who is driving which car has gotten complicated." I shook my head, glancing up and down the driveway. "But where would they go?"

Beth rubbed her eyes. "I'm worried, Hudson's catheter incision isn't healed yet; he shouldn't strain himself."

"Well, where would they go? It's the middle of the night."

Mindy let out a hard, gusty exhale. "So much happens in the middle of the night for us."

I tried not to grin, but she was right. "Wait, did Colt give Hudson the old baseball today? I'd found it in the house, and he ran home to show Hudson."

"He did. And Hudson told him a story about how he threw his baseballs at the raccoons that came onto the property. How he climbed his fort at night, and waited, and then he used baseballs as cannons."

I whispered, "I know where they are. Come with me. But be quiet and listen." We snuck from beneath her carport, standing next to the fence of my backyard, and I pointed up at the tree. "Listen."

Mindy got closer to me. "What are we doing?"

"We're about to catch a couple of raccoons."

Tee-hee-hee. Tee-hee-hee.

Mindy glanced up, pointing with both hands. "They're in your tree, aren't they?"

"Yes, follow me. Let's get them."

We rushed down the fence line, into my yard, and Mindy unscrewed the sprinkler from the hose. She ran to the oak tree. "Beth, turn the water on. And do it now!"

I hesitated. "But Hudson can't strain himself."

"That's too bad. If he can climb a tree, then he deserves this!"

I twisted the nozzle, the water gushing forth, and Mindy held her fingers over the end, spraying water up to the fort. "So, are there any raccoons up there? You'd better get down before you fall. I've had it with you both!"

Tee-hee-hee.

I ran to Mindy's side, taking the hose from her. "Let me show you how to spray water." I put two fingers on the end, forcing the spray higher into the tree.

Colt yelled, "Daddy, they've found us."

"You're right. We're staying here. It's a flood of angry women down below."

Mindy chuckled, "Both of you get down here. Hudson Henry Hinkle and Colt Carson Hinkle, if you two don't get down from the tree right now, I'm coming up for you.

Colt stuck his head out from the fort. "Daddy, we'd better go. Mommy used our middle names."

In minutes, the raccoons descended, and Hudson laughed with his son and wife in my backyard—a familiar sound—one I hadn't heard from him in twenty years.

I moved to turn off the water, but Colt, in his pajamas, yanked the hose from my grasp, spraying me down. "You invaded our fort. We claim it back."

Mindy snatched the hose from Colt, and in seconds, she and Colt rolled on the ground in the grass. Hudson rushed away from them and moved to one of the chairs on the porch, holding his stomach—but laughing like years of joy escaped from his belly.

I joined him. I whispered, "You used to sit there when you were ten. It's been a while."

Hudson held his stomach. "I probably shouldn't have climbed that tree, but sometimes when things seem lost, you have to find your way back up the tree."

Somehow, what he said made sense. "Hudson, I'm so sorry for everything. I can't change the past, but will you please let me be your aunt again?"

Hudson stretched his hand across the patio table. "You've always been my aunt. I just haven't been a good nephew."

I took his hand. "Well, certain things are not really lost. We were bound to find each other again—like raccoons in the night."

"Thank you for saving my toys. I don't have many tangible things from my childhood. But one thing I know, I was free over here—on days when my dad was too loud. Thank you for giving me a safe place to come."

"You're welcome. Your dad and Rhett came from some hard places of their own—it's too bad they got lost in their anger."

"Yes, I'm not going to be like my dad. Well, I am some. He had good parts; not everything he did was horrible. I want to capture some great memories with Colt, no matter how many days I have left."

I turned the water off next to the porch. "Well, it looks like your family needs a bath."

"I think you're right! At least the fort didn't fall."

A crackling sound popped, as the walls of the fort tumbled from the tree, landing in a pile on the grass. Colt yelled, "Daddy's fort is gone."

I held Hudson's hand. "But oh, the memory of watching you and your dad in the tree—that's something Monopoly money can't buy.

A TOUCH OF GRACE

The *Back-To-School Program,* with a Sunday night meal of chicken spaghetti, salad, and garlic toast, drew more than 100 people. Gladys put her team of cooks together and created a feast.

At our round table, Marty sat next to me, with Stanley, Gladys, and, of course, Reed. The most actual miracle of the night was having Hudson with us.

Colt slapped his garlic bread on his plate. "I don't like the taste of garlic. It's yucky."

Mindy corrected Colt. "Will you stop that? We don't hit the table with our food."

Hudson grinned. "Colt, listen to your mother."

"Yes, sir." Colt put the garlic bread on the tablecloth and pushed it as far as he could.

I stood up, announcing, "Well, it's time to get my kiddos ready. We've got to warm up."

Colt jumped up, knocking his folding chair to the floor. "Sorry." He picked up the chair. "I'm ready to sing."

Hudson scooted Colt's chair closer. "You'll do great, Son."

I ushered Colt along, waving at several of the other children as we crossed the fellowship room. I held Colt's hand. "I can't wait to hear you all sing."

In the chapel off the main sanctuary, we went through the verses and songs. First, we sang "I Have Decided to Follow Jesus," then "My God is So Big," and finally "This Little Light of Mine." Then, for our final number, Holly and Colt performed their song "Amazing Grace," and I backed them up on the chorus.

"Everyone, ready or not, here we come. Let's make a joyful noise tonight. You've worked for weeks on your music. I can't wait for your parents to see how great you sing."

I led the children in prayer, and we took our place in the choir loft, and the seats in the sanctuary filled up with moms and dads, friends and neighbors, along with grandmas and papaws. Every year, plenty of relatives attend the fundraiser to help provide backpacks for every student at the church.

I sat at the end of the front row in the loft, snapping my fingers at two boys, then a girl, and then making goofy faces that made them all giggle. To say I'm blessed is an understatement. I have more children in my life than should be allowed.

As the pews filled, the children fidgeted but, for the most part, remained quiet. We were ready to sing with taped music, and the music man sat in the balcony at the sound system, waiting for his cue. We had the cadence down, the words memorized, and the hand motions perfected.

The adult choir took the stage in front of us, standing like robots. They'll sing a few songs, and the pastor will brag on those who helped with the fundraiser, and he'll tell everyone how the backpacks will be dispersed.

I wiggled with the kids, waited for our turn, got lost in the moment, and then I saw Marty off to my right, between two men in the choir. His ruddy skin, brown hair, and bright eyes were glued to me. And he waved.

Cindy Sue, who sat next to me, giggled. "I think that man's smiling at you."

I argued, "No man would ever think of smiling at me."

"Well, he is." Cindy Sue waved back, making the girls sitting near her laugh. Lindsey, two seats over, giggled. "Ms. Beth has a boyfriend."

"Girls, we're in church. Behave."

Colt was behind me and leaned forward. "Ms. Beth, Marty's waving at you."

I slipped from the platform, and Marty came my way. "What is it? You're a distraction. Even my kids are noticing you."

"Well, that's good. I need you to know that Hudson's sick. His head's hurting, and Mindy is considering taking him home. But he's insisting on staying. Just don't tell Colt if he leaves— Mindy wants Colt to sing, no matter what."

"No, I pray Hudson gets to stay."

"I just thought you should know."

"Okay, thanks. The program's about to start. Maybe he'll get to hear Colt."

I slid to the choir loft like a raccoon, hoping no one noticed, but since I was the only person moving on the platform, I knew that was nearly impossible.

Cindy Sue asked, "Is he your boyfriend, for real?"

"He's a friend. That's all."

The following minutes felt like days. The adults sang—yes, every single blasted verse in all their songs. The pastor got wound up, turning his greeting and announcements into a mini sermon with not three points but five.

My kids wiggled, and someone pinched Nancy, who hit Carl. Then Penny slipped out of her chair, and the boys laughed at her. Tina, who sat four seats from me, hummed and made bumblebee sounds. And soon, David was using his cast as a drum. I was surrounded by a hornet's nest of stingers, not singers.

The attention span of my group was beyond over, and I joined them. I didn't see Hudson or Mindy in the sanctuary, which didn't help me sit still or behave either. I'm moving around more than my kids. Then Colt tapped my shoulder. "Where's my mom and dad? I don't see them."

"I'm sure they're out there. It's crowded." I assured Colt, but Marty's gaze told me they were not in the sanctuary.

The time came for our three songs, and I moved to the pulpit. "Hello, everyone. Our children will take you on a road trip now. We're going to sing about a life that follows Jesus, trusting God since He's bigger than our problems. And we'll then sing about how God is the light to our journey. Our fourth and final song will spotlight two youngsters, Holly Friday and Colt Hinkle, as they sing about God's amazing grace."

I motioned to the soundman and to the children to stand. Their eyes grew wide, their attention serious, and several wore panicked expressions.

The music filled the sanctuary, and the children opened their mouths. A chorus of beauty radiated from them as they received applause between each song. And by the middle of the third number, their harmonies kicked in, and the angelic sound was better than any rehearsal.

"Colt and Holly. Please step forward and close out our night." Holly scooted to her spot at a mic, while Colt floundered his way to his designated place. His eyes were searching for

Hudson and Mindy. I, too, hoped they were somewhere in the crowd.

I gave the sound man a cue with my hand, and Holly chimed in; her face froze with a glare at Colt because he didn't sing with her.

I stepped up. "Let's try this again. Are you both ready?"

Colt nodded. Holly sighed.

The tune played over the sound system, but only Holly sang. She threw up her hands, shouting into the mic. "Colt Hinkle. This is a duet. Sing with me. Or I'm leaving."

"I'm trying to sing. But nothing will come out."

From the back of the sanctuary, a man's voice called, "I'll sing with you, Colt."

Hudson made a slow march down the aisle to the platform. He bent down to speak into the microphone. "I'll make this a trio. But I don't think we need any music." He turned to Holly. "Will you sing with Colt and me?"

Holly sniffled and nodded. "I'll sing with you."

Colt took his dad's hand. "I'll sing too."

I moved to the pulpit, retrieved another microphone, and handed it to Hudson.

He sighed, "I may never get this chance again. Sometimes, it's time to sing. Sometimes, it's time to climb trees. And sometimes, it's a time to forgive and live."

I wiped the stream of tears from my face, and Marty motioned for me to come sit down front with him. So, like a puppy in training, I joined Marty, and we were right in front of Hudson, Colt, and Holly. Then Mindy slipped into the pew with us.

Hudson took a deep breath. "Colt, start us out. I need a little help."

Colt uttered a weak sound, but Holly joined him, and they sang, "Amazing grace, how sweet the sound that saved a wretch like me. I once was lost, but now I'm found. Was blind but now I see."

In seconds, the children stood and sang along, followed by the adult choir, which returned to the stage.

A man sat at the end of my row, his calloused hands and sun-scorched skin—it was my neighbor, the one I first hired to take down my fence and to build the fort, the one I fired. He was the very man whose wife had slipped away to Arizona, and now, he was in church, and I was thrilled.

Maybe if he allows God to rescue and deliver and have His way, there could be hope for his marriage. There could be hope for this man to live in peace. And for his wife. Maybe.

The beauty of the moment unleashed a flood of emotions, and then the man with the secrets knelt at the altar, weeping. And our pastor came alongside the man to pray with him.

Hudson pointed at me, motioning for me to come to the platform. "It's time for all of you to hear from Beth Bender, a voice of hope for this community."

I stepped to the mic and spoke. "Friends, it's been a long time. But let's go through the song once more—and close out in prayer."

Hudson inched his way to the altar with Mindy by his side. And Colt knelt by his dad. Then Marty found his place on his knees as did dozens of other people as I sang, "Amazing grace, how sweet the sound, that saved a wretch like me."

The rest of the night became a blur of hugs and tears and letting go of fears—of finding my song of praise once more.

Soon, I felt a hand on my shoulder as I knelt at the altar too, and I turned to see the face of friendship. "Sally? I didn't know if you'd made it."

"Yes, I wouldn't have missed this for the world."

Pearson grinned, as if he were the happiest man in town. "Can we pray for you? You've touched so many lives. We will forever be your friend."

I nodded, unable to speak, and soon, Marty found his way next to me, too. I whispered to him at the altar. "I think I'll go on that date with you."

Marty smiled, "Is this what you do at the altar? You make dates with people who pray for you?"

"Well, yes, sometimes, I do."

Later, as the red, blue, and purple backpacks were given out, I thought about all the ups and downs in my life. About the locks and fences and harshness and surviving—and how through it all God guided me.

Sometimes life is turned on high and floods the street with pain and sorrow. And at other times, it's refreshing and all about rebuilding. Whatever I water will grow in my yard and in my heart. When I truly trust Jesus, He quenches my weary soul, even with mango tea. Then I can find a way to tear down the fence of my past and live!

TOENAIL MONSTERS

It's been three weeks since school started, and Colt calls me from his new treehouse most afternoons when I'm sitting on my patio.

I moved across the grass, my bare feet tender, so I walked slowly and purposefully. I waved to Colt as he stood in the doorway of his fort. "Hi there, sweet boy. You left your wiffle balls over here and your bat. I've found your basketball, too. And your crocs."

He yelled, "Can I come over?"

"If your mom and dad say it's okay." I brushed my hair from my eyes. "But don't you have homework?"

"Mom had me do it when she picked me up. She told me that Daddy isn't good at making me do my homework when she's at work with you."

"Well, I hope to see you in a few minutes." I turned to go back to the patio.

Colt yelled, "Hey, look! There's a butterfly. It's right by the driveway. I think it's the same one we saw when I fell from your tree."

I nodded. "I bet it's another one. They don't live all that long." I marched across my yard to Colt's backyard—the fence of my past long gone. Our yards are now connected.

Colt interrupted my thoughts. "Hey, Ms. Beth, I see butterflies above your head. There's one, two, three. Wait, four."

I now stood beneath the ladder leading up the tree to the rocket fort, which hovered about five feet from the ground. Colt wanted his dad to be able to climb up, especially on days when Hudson was weak, so the fort was lowered by six feet.

I smiled. "I guess we've got a butterfly family today."

Colt hollered, "I have a family, too. My mom. My dad. Harry. Beauty. And you!"

"Me? So, I'm family?"

"Yeah, even if you're too old to climb trees."

And with that, I tore up the ladder. "Wait, until I get you, Colt Hinkle. I'm going to tickle you until you scream."

Colt laughed, "But don't let me fall from the tree."

"I won't. I'll catch you if you fall." Inside the treehouse, a ragged piece of paper hung by one of the windows. "Who is that?"

"I drew her. She's an angel."

"Wow, that's a great drawing."

"I did it during math at school."

I laughed. "During math? Aren't you supposed to be listening to the teacher?"

"Yeah, but I was already finished with my math. So, I drew an angel."

I remarked, "She has big blue eyes."

Colt nodded. "Yeah, like you."

"She has bangs like me, too."

He pointed. "She keeps her hair in her eyes like you, too."

I swiped mine to the side. "But what is she standing by?"

"Oh, this angel has water sprinklers. Lots of them."

"So, it's an angel with hair and bangs like me. And water sprinklers like me."

"Yeah, you have too many water sprinklers."

I argued, "But I'm no angel?"

Colt touched the drawing. "Mommy says you are. She said some angels live right next door—and that sometimes they have a name."

"Your mom is pretty smart—but I'm just a regular woman living next door to you." I wiggled my toes, hovering near the ladder. "So, what's your angel's name?"

"Oh, it's Beth."

"Well, as I said, I'm no angel."

"I know—but you might be someday. But I don't think people get to be angels. They do other stuff for God."

I laughed, "Well, are you coming over to my house or not?"

"No, you're here now. Let's play with my marbles while I wait for Lucas to show up. He's coming for supper. It was Daddy's idea."

I caught my toe on the ladder. "Oh, guess what? The toenail monsters are gone. I haven't seen one in weeks."

"Ms. Beth, you know there's no such thing as a toenail monster?"

"What makes you so sure? We've jumped over them this past month, remember? And you still have your toenails."

Colt glanced at my feet. "Ms. Beth, have you looked at your toes? Your toenails—they're gross."

"Silly boy, that's nail polish—it's forest green. Not a fungus."

We laughed and laughed, tossing cat eyes against the fort's wall. Above us, butterflies applauded our joy—their beautiful wings a reminder of what life is like serving God.

Now there's a fresh scent of hope—at the old Hinkle house—and mine.

I no longer have cameras on my house or three locks per door, and my car is running again—and Stanley's on the mend. Reed is planning and managing the station, even though, for now, Stanley's still working with us there.

Colt tapped my arm. "It's your turn. Roll your marble."

I tossed my marble like an angel might, soft and precise. "Look there; I'm winning." I hugged Colt, teasing him with my silliness. "Hey, did you know I'm singing at church Sunday morning?"

"Mom said you were doing it for Marty."

"So, do you eavesdrop on every conversation?"

"Not all of them. Just the ones I can hear."

"Well, I'm singing 'His Eye Is on the Sparrow.'"

"I think you should sing 'His Eye is on the Butterfly.'"

I giggled. "I don't know that song."

Colt chimed in with his version. "Jesus is my portion; a constant friend is He. His eye is on the butterfly. And I know He watches over me."

I hugged Colt. "Now, you know that's not how I'll sing it. Hey, you could sing the hymn with me if you want. The right way."

"Nope, I can't. I'm saving my singing for when Daddy comes again and when he can sing."

I sighed. "I hope and pray that's real soon, Colt. I really do."

"Me, too." Colt stuck his head out the fort window. "There's Daddy now. Daddy, Ms. Beth is in the fort. She doesn't fit too well."

I hung my head out the fort's door. "Hey there, Hudson. Is today a good day?"

"Yes, ma'am. Every day I'm above the ground is a good day."

Colt yelled. "Well, Ms. Beth says the toenail monsters are gone. So, we're safe!"

Hudson moved slower than slow, his skin pale. "I'll climb up there soon. And we'll become raccoons again—and hide from your mom."

From behind Hudson, Mindy called, "I know where you two go to hide." She wrapped her fingers around Hudson's hand.

I bellowed from the tree. "I'm so thankful for all three of you—you're the family God knew I needed. Life is mostly ordinary, and then one day someone…."

Hudson nodded. "You mean me?"

I smiled. "Yes, I mean you. Someone bursts into life as a small boy, only for loss to send him away to live in a cocoon for years. And then, like a blaze of color and in an utterly extraordinary way, God stepped in and changed everything."

Mindy added, "This past month has been the longest—and the shortest and holds the greatest importance in many ways. It shows me how empowering change can be when God speaks to a life."

Hudson sniffled. "Again, you mean me."

"Yes, honey. I have watched how God transformed you in this short time. It's giving me hope."

Hudson nodded and embraced Mindy. "I ran from my past when my future was waiting for me right here."

I swung my feet to the ladder of the fort and missed the rung. "Oh, my word! I'm slipping!" And with that, I thudded to the ground, rolling like a woman too old to be climbing trees—one now moaning. I was never so thankful for the rocket fort being so close to the ground.

Hudson rushed to my side. "Are you hurt?"

"Only my pride. Only my pride."

Colt yelled from above. "See, if you were an angel, you wouldn't have hit the ground—because you would know how to fly."

I unfolded from the ground. "My wings are in the dryer—I just washed them, or I would have soared high into the sky."

Mindy laughed. "I don't think wings were meant to be tossed into a dryer."

Colt laughed, "She doesn't have wings. Remember, she's not a real angel."

Hudson leaned in close to my ear, brushing dirt from my sleeve. "To me, you're an angel. And I owe you everything."

I held Hudson close. "We sure did go around the world to find each other, but I'm so blessed that you made your way home."

A silver car pulled up beside my house, a woman at the wheel. She parked, waved at me, and ran toward me. "It's me, Addy Alistair. I came back from Arizona to tell you something and say it to your face."

I squinted. "Addy? You look so tan. And healthy."

"I'm doing great. Just great. I'm still processing what's happened these last few years, but I'm not afraid anymore. I came back to see my mother in Texarkana—to tell her what happened and where I had disappeared. I've only called once to tell her I'm safe, so I know she's been worried."

"And you came to see me?"

"Yes, I had to."

I smiled. "I'm thankful for how you look in the daylight, too! Your glow is back." I wiped dirt from my pants.

Addy reached into her tote. "I wanted to give you this." She held out a small box with a yellow bow.

"What? It's not my birthday or anything."

"You don't understand. You saved my life! Literally. Without that phone call. Without your insistence on picking me up. Without the hotel. And the plane ticket. I'd be trapped in that violent world."

I opened the box, pulling a silver necklace from inside the silk cloth. I assured her, "Only Jesus can pull us from the wasteland to the treehouse of hope again." I held up my gift. "It's a necklace with angel wings. Look, Colt. I do have wings!"

Colt called from the fort. "Now you can fly!"

I soaked in the confirmation that helping others is my calling, and in Addy's eyes, I saw a glimpse of what God meant to a life. Because all my life, I've been carried by His grace. God rescued me when I was three, when my parents left me. And His grace allowed me to be a child with Hudson when he played in my yard, once as a boy, again as a man-raccoon.

Mindy asked, "Would anyone like some mango tea? It seems to cure what ails us." She moved to the door.

Addy remarked, "If you're offering, I'd love a glass of tea!"

"I'll bring the pitcher and glasses out. I'll be right back."

I took Addy's hand. "Thank you so much. Let's enjoy this moment. Seeing you is like a treasure for my shoebox."

Addy smiled. "Shoebox?"

Colt called from the fort. "It's where we save the important things."

Hudson pulled up a patio chair in the shade of his tree, watching his son. "I'll sit here."

I paused, glancing up to the fort, inhaling, and wiggling my toes. I whispered to God, "Thank you for giving me a reason to sing."

Mindy rushed back to the yard, gasping like a puppy. "Baylor just called. Hudson is getting his transplants!"

Summertime Sprinkler

Sometimes the best view comes from climbing up a tree to a rocket fort, or it can show up at ground level, too, when the phone rings or when a car drives up, or on those days when you remember playing in a water sprinkler.

Pam Kumpe

Books by Pam Kumpe
<u>Annie Grace Kree Chronicles Series</u>
1 Untied Shoelace
2 Unknown Soul
3 Rescue of Undaunted Spirit
4 Unwanted Sidekick
5 Unwavering Hope
6 Unshackled Courage

<u>Other Novels</u>
Rescue at Three Sisters Springs
Looking for Daddy's Girl
Where Horses Run Secrets Hide

<u>Devotional</u>
Looking for Daddy's Girl Devotional
See You in the Funny Papers
A Scoop of Inspiration
You Are Not A Typo

<u>Young Reader Chapter Books</u>
The Mystery of Sneaky Pants
The Mystery of Sneak Paws
The Mystery of the Sneaky Parrots
The Mystery of Sneaky Dill Pickens
Of Parrots, Prank, and Prayers (Devotional)

Children
In the Lick of Time
A Goat with a Tote
Hattie Holmes Holds Her Breath
Hattie and Mattie! Oh, They Love the Bunny!
Cranky Camel and the Candy Cane Caper
Cranky Camel and Barnyard's God Talent
Cranky the Camel and Max Go To School
Spike's Glow

Rehab Ministry
Things I Learned in Jail
From Court to Christ

Bible Study
Think Outside the Pit Workbook
Think Outside the Pit Devotional

Homeless Ministry
My View from the Bridge
My View from the Street
My View of the Heart

www.pamkumpe.com